D0323379

DISAPPEAR HOME

DISAPPEAR HOME

LAURA HURWITZ

Albert Whitman & Company
Chicago, Illinois

Library of Congress Cataloging-in-Publication data
is on file with the publisher.

Text copyright © 2015 by Laura Hurwitz
Published in 2015 by Albert Whitman & Company
ISBN 978-0-8075-2468-8
All rights reserved. No part of this book may be reproduced or transmitted
in any form or by any means, electronic or mechanical, including
photocopying, recording, or by any information storage and retrieval
system, without permission in writing from the publisher.

Printed in China.
10 9 8 7 6 5 4 3 2 1 NP 20 19 18 17 16 15 14

Cover design by Jordan Kost
Cover image © Jessica Islam Lia/Getty Images

For more information about Albert Whitman & Company,
visit our web site at www.albertwhitman.com.

3 1327 00597 2922

For my mother

Shoshanna knew evil when it crossed her path. Hell, she had walked with it by her side, whispering like a serpent in her ear, for nearly fifteen years. She and Ella knew that time had run out. The time to think maybe next month, next week had passed. What came next had to be stopped. They had to leave. Now.

She was terrified. She wasn't ready. She also knew, in this moment, as she stood there, face impassive, weighing the unknown against something horribly certain, that they had no choice. They would choose the unknown. It was their only hope.

CHAPTER ONE

The year was 1972; the month, June. Alongside the car, the full moon seemed to be chasing them, flying along the telephone wires, slicing through the tops of the trees. Closing her eyes, Shoshanna rested her head against the cool metal of the car door. They had been driving since early morning, stopping twice— once for gas, and once so that she and Mara could pee, squatting uncomfortably in the brambly scrub grass behind a tree at the side of the road. She couldn't figure out which ached worse, her head or her stomach. How long had it been since they'd eaten? There was that bowl of granola for breakfast, but she'd had to dump it over the porch rail because the milk was clotted and sour.

Mara was asleep, slumped sideways like a rag doll, her tangle of gold hair spilled across the seat, rib cage rising and falling with each soft, snuffly breath. Shoshanna touched her fingertips to her sister's shoulder. Mara stirred slightly, scratched her nose, and murmured something about pancakes before sliding back into sleep.

Shoshanna knew not to ask her mother where they were going or how much longer they would be driving. She turned to look at the moon again. So, this was freedom. She could hardly believe it. After months of conspiring, they had escaped. Never mind that Sweet Earth Farm—clinging like a burr to the outskirts of Cave Junction, Oregon, population just under two thousand— had been the only home she'd known for the past five years, since just before she turned ten.

Never mind that this meant leaving her father, Adam, who just the other day had stared into her eyes, the same deep, unfathomable brown as his, and told her that she would be nothing if not for him. He gave her life. Never mind that the three of them were making their escape from Sweet Earth with hardly any money and no long-term plan. The fact was, she knew that they would be better off just about anyplace else, because with the ever-presents—the hunger, the violence, the drugs, the chaos—things had gotten badly out of hand.

Shoshanna, Ellen, and Mara had long harbored the intention of escaping. At night, hunkered down on their lumpy mattress (found abandoned on the side of the road outside Portland; they considered themselves lucky), the three of them whispered sedition before falling asleep. During the day, they hatched and re-hatched plans in the orchard when they were alone, sorting and crating apples while the other Sweet Earthers smoked dope in the clearing just down the hill.

Southern California, Ella told her daughters, was the land of sunshine, orange groves, and Disneyland. To Shoshanna and Mara, southern California sounded like paradise. How could life be anything other than perfect in a place like that? But first, they had to get out, which was not going to be an easy thing to pull off.

For one thing, Sweet Earth Farm was smack-dab in the middle of nowhere. It was thirty miles to Grants Pass, the nearest real town with shops and a post office and a library—thirty hilly and perilous miles at that, bumping along a rutted, narrow road. There were only two working vehicles at the commune: the ancient pickup truck they used to bring Sweet Earth's crop of organic apples to the farmers' market on the weekends, and the station wagon. Anyone who wanted to use the wagon had to ask days in advance and most of the time had to share it with Sweet Earthers going roughly the same direction at roughly the same time.

Shoshanna remembered when she'd gone into Grants Pass with Adam and eleven other people and two dogs. Adam needed a hash pipe, so she went along for the ride, all of them packed into the car like sweat- and patchouli-scented sardines. They were let out in front of a dilapidated house that doubled as a makeshift head shop. The others went about their various errands and started back to the farm, forgetting Shoshie and Adam, who had to wait outside in the rain, chilled to the bone and miserable, for four hours, which was how long it took for the others to get home and realize they'd left them behind. Adam had been so pissed off that he kicked a hole in the car door and didn't speak to anyone for two weeks.

But today, so far, the Plan seemed to be working. The particulars of their exit came to Ella seemingly overnight. One morning she told them to get ready, that they'd be leaving in two days. She had all figured it out. Ella told the others that she had to take the girls to the free clinic in Ashland because they had worms. She told the girls to scratch their butts in the meantime, for the sake of authenticity, and both girls set to scratching with dramatic gusto.

No one on the commune wanted worms, so they were quick to tell Ella to take the car and keep the girls the hell away from them. Ella promised to have the car back by noon. They would stir up suspicion by packing, so Shoshanna and Mara put two extra layers of clothes on under what they were wearing and grabbed any small items that they couldn't bear to leave. They didn't have much.

Mara took her pink blanket and a small, pink vinyl pocketbook with a broken clasp, crammed with old crayons, elastic bands, and some bits of brightly colored turquoise and lapis lazuli left over from the jewelry Ella made. Shoshanna had an ancient, illustrated copy of Kipling's *Just So Stories* that had been dumped into the trash after the flea market a few weeks before and an intricately tooled leather barrette, left behind by a teenybopper who was just passing through. At the last minute, she grabbed a color snapshot of their family from four years before, when things were maybe not okay, but better. She was standing and Adam was behind her, his sinewy arms wrapped tight around her, his bearded face resting on her head, and Mara was a chubby towheaded toddler safe in Ella's arms. That was it.

Ella packed a paper bag with contraband: a whole loaf of bread and a jar of peanut butter and half a box of raisins. She even filled an old milk carton with water and left it under a bush next to the car, with the intention of throwing everything in at the last minute when no one was looking. But when Reed and Alex, two of the newer members of Sweet Earth, walked toward the car as she and the girls were trying to get in, she knew she couldn't risk it. Food was scarce at Sweet Earth Farm. Shoshie had once heard Adam threaten to cut off some guy's hand because he'd taken a bag of potatoes. (According to Adam, "That's what they do in Thailand, man.")

Even a small amount was not something you could casually walk away with. They would have to eat at some point though, and Shoshanna could see the panic in her mother's eyes, followed by feverish survival strategizing. Keeping her voice calm, casual, she asked Reed and Alex for money to cover the doctor's visit ("Do you have any bread on you? Adam's good for it. I just need a couple of dollars, man."), but they shook their heads, snorting derisively.

"The clinic's not called 'the free clinic' for nothing. Do you think they expect you to *pay*? Damn, Adam's right. You are a stupid cow." That's what Reed said, looking into the backseat at the two girls. His gaze lingered on Shoshanna, who played with the lid of the ashtray, while Mara gave her butt a theatrical scratch.

"Yeah. I guess so." Ella looked away. Shoshanna had watched her mother stop standing up for herself a long time ago. She understood. Back talk led to trouble. Ella got in, shutting the door on her long, gauzy skirt, then sighed as she reopened the door, rescued the skirt, and slammed it shut again. "Okay. Ready, girls?" She turned to look at them with a mix of terror and triumph, and in that look they felt the full weight of the moment. Turning back around, squaring her shoulders, and taking a deep breath, she started the car.

"So, you say you're gonna be back by noon?" Reed shouted over the noise of the engine. He pulled a cigarette from his pocket and motioned for Ella to hand him the lighter from the dashboard.

"Yeah." The lighter popped out, coils glowing, and she handed it to him, waiting as he took a drag and exhaled extravagantly into the open window, into her face. She waited for the smoke to clear before answering. "Maybe before. I guess it depends on if there's a wait at the clinic."

"If the line's too long, forget it. Melaya probably knows some kind of homeopathic way to get rid of worms. She's into that kind of herbal remedy shit. She's supposed to be back from Corvallis tomorrow. We just need the car soon, man. Will has to get into town when he comes down from his acid trip to score some peyote for Adam, and you don't need me to tell you that it's not a good idea to keep Adam waiting to get high. Man, *worms*. Bummer, huh?"

He looked at Shoshanna again, eyes traveling from her dark brown hair to her long, field-tanned legs. "Hey, Shosh, maybe this'll teach you to keep your fingers out of your ass." Alex grinned. "You too, Sunshine." That's what everyone at Sweet Earth called Mara, "Sunshine," because of her wild yellow hair and ear-to-ear grin.

"Uh-huh," Shoshanna murmured. Reed gave her an uneasy feeling that started in the pit of her stomach and traveled up her spine. She did her best to avoid him. Now that the engine had started, Shoshanna felt bold enough to look at both Reed and Alex straight on, to see them for what they were: two skinny-hipped, thin-lipped, squinty-eyed lowlifes in patched jeans and dirty work boots. She was thinking that if she never saw them again in her life, it would be too soon. Her mother backed the station wagon out, then turned and drove slowly down the rutted dirt road. None of them looked back. They sat staring straight ahead, silent, holding their breath until Ella turned the wheel sharply right and they were on the paved road. "Do you think we're going to be okay, Ma?" Shoshanna asked, her voice a whisper.

"I think so. If the car doesn't break down. We have enough gas to go a decent distance. Three quarters of a tank—that's better than I expected. I have ten dollars here that we can use to buy more."

Mara let out a huge whoop. "We're free, we're free!"

"Shhh," Ella said, but she was smiling too. "Adam has radar." Suddenly, she let out a big whoop herself. "O-*kay*. Man, it does feel good, doesn't it? Real scary, but real good. My heart is pounding. Damn." She shook her head and started laughing. "If they find us, they'll kill us."

Shoshanna shook her head. "Nah. What do they care? Yesterday Adam told me and Mara that the dog was worth more than us two put together. He wasn't even talking about the new dog. He meant the old one with the goopy eye and three legs. No one's gonna miss us at all, Ma. Not Adam. Not anyone."

"They might not miss us, but they'll sure as hell miss the station wagon." She laughed, popped in the cigarette lighter, and shuffled around in her worn canvas knapsack for her Marlboros. Shoshanna noticed that her mother's fingers were shaking. Lighting up, she sucked in a lungful and exhaled, then tapped the steering wheel nervously. "We have our work cut out for us, girls. We have our work cut out. I think you two better sit back. I'm just going to keep on driving."

Eight hours later found them on the interstate somewhere in southern Oregon, traveling south through the night, destination unknown. Shoshanna looked out the window and saw only the road ahead, the moon rising overhead, and dusk beginning to settle on either side. Her mother yawned.

"Are you tired, Ma?"

"Yeah."

"Maybe we should pull over somewhere, so that you can rest your eyes or something."

"Yeah. That's not a bad idea. I'm about to pass out. We have to find someplace where the cops won't hassle us, though. Maybe we should take the next exit and see if we can find someplace to stop for the night."

Turning off the highway, she paused at the end of the ramp. To the left or to the right? Either direction looked equally dark and foreboding. "What do you think, Shosh? I'm not getting any vibes here."

Ella and Shoshanna believed in vibes. They believed in vibes like other people believe in God. Shoshanna closed her eyes and tried to feel something. "Go right."

"Okay, baby." The road was lined with towering pine trees on either side, and Shoshanna was beginning to question the accuracy of the vibes when finally the woods came to an end and a cluster of one-story buildings appeared. There were streetlights and a gas station, a row of shops and a small wooden building that she figured was a church since it had a steeple. Ella turned into the church's driveway and circled around to the back parking lot.

Aside from an overflowing dumpster, the lot was empty. "This looks like a good place to stop. You can't see the car from the road. We'll take off when the sun comes up."

It felt good to stop moving. Ella curled up in the front seat, knees braced against the steering wheel, and Shoshanna tucked herself alongside Mara, who continued to slumber soundly. "Night, Ma."

"Night."

"Ma?"

"Ummm?" Ella murmured, hovering on the blurry divide between waking and sleeping.

"Are you scared?"

"Yeah."

"Scared that they're going to catch us?"

"That, and I'm scared that we're close to broke and we have no food, and I don't know where I'm going or what I'm going to do when I get there."

"Don't worry, Ma. It'll be okay. Don't you remember the Plan? The *Plan*. Drive south to California. First San Francisco, then Los Angeles. Disneyland, oranges, beaches, and sunshine. Remember?"

"Yeah. I remember." Ella sounded suddenly fretful. "It's just—I don't know, Shoshie. I just gotta get us there. *I* gotta get us there. It's me that has to get us through the day-to-day part, in this junky car with no money.

Planning is one thing. It's fun. It's like make-believe. This is life. This is real."

"I can help you, Ma. You know that. I always do." But Ella had already fallen asleep.

Shoshanna thought about what her mother had said. The day-to-day part. That this was real. What had sounded like a wonderful adventure, their whispered words lying in bed at Sweet Earth, now sounded tedious and difficult. Even worse, it sounded like something Ella wasn't sure she could do. Shoshie knew she'd have to work hard to keep her mother going. She also knew there was no going back. She had watched Adam kick a dent in the car door. She had watched him do other things that were way worse.

✳ ✳ ✳

It seemed as if Shoshanna had just closed her eyes when she felt Mara tugging at her shoulder. The rising sun painted the worn gray upholstery shades of apricot and gold. "I'm hungry, Shosh," Mara whined. "Thirsty too. I keep thinking about pancakes."

Shoshanna struggled to sit up. Where they, anyway? Looking out the window, she saw the church, which was a ramshackle sight in the harsh light of day, with its peeling paint and sign that said "Divin avior

Methodi urch. Spen your unday with s." The parking lot was still empty. She could see the backyards of small, boxy houses with sagging clotheslines and chain-link fences. They were a good distance away, beyond the edges of the parking lot and across a set of overgrown railroad tracks.

"Look, Mare," she said, making her voice sound much more enthusiastic than she was feeling. "We're in a cute little town. Maybe we can stop somewhere and get something to eat."

"My tummy hurts," said Mara. "I'm so hungry. I don't like this."

"I know. Me too, Mare. Ma?" Shoshanna leaned over the seat and poked her mother's back gingerly. "Ma? I know you're tired but it's morning. We got to get going."

Ella groaned and sat up, smacking her elbow on the steering wheel. "Ow. Damn." She rubbed her elbow and looked out the window. "Where do you think we are? This is still Oregon, right?"

"I guess so. We're in a church parking lot."

"I'm hungry, Ma," whined Mara. "And thirsty."

"Yeah, I know, Mare. Join the club. Only problem is, I don't have any money. Not for food, anyway. All I have is the ten bucks I'm gonna need for gas. Hey, look on the floor and in the seats. Maybe there's some change or something." They searched, wedging their fingers into the gully between the seat bottom and the seat back, scouring the gritty, sticky floor, snapping open every ashtray. They found thirty-six cents plus a Canadian nickel that they might be able to use if some store clerk wasn't paying close attention.

"Not bad." Ella seemed to perk up slightly. "We should be able to get something with that. We'll stop at the next gas station to use the bathroom and get some water. Gas stations usually have vending machines. We can pick up a couple of candy bars or something."

"Candy bars!" Mara bounced up and down on the seat, the worn springs making a braying donkey sound. *Hee-haw, hee-haw.* Generally, Ella didn't allow them to have chocolate or refined sugar, but it seemed to Shoshanna that on the road, especially on the road to freedom, all rules had been thrown out the window.

"Just this once, Mare. I think we all could use a sugar high, but just for today."

"All right!" Mara bounced up and down. "Three Musketeers!"

Ella shook her head but she was grinning at the same time. "You are a junk-food junkie. I'm guessing the junk will get us through the morning, but then we're going to have to get some serious food. I hate to say it, but I'll have to count on you two for that."

Shoshanna's stomach flip-flopped. She knew what her mother meant. Years ago, when they still lived in San Francisco, Adam taught her something he called "family fun and games." The three of them would go into a store, and while Ella and Adam bought a couple of dollars' worth of stuff at one end of an aisle, Shoshanna would grab many times that amount of stuff at the opposite end, hiding it in her pockets and under her shirt. Adam figured that if she got caught, which she occasionally did, he would stage a big public display of paternal outrage. This included yelling, a lecture on morality, and a very real, painful, and humiliating spanking.

Most of the time, though, she got away with it, and their success record improved when later, Mara joined the game. Not that it was anything to be proud of, but they were excellent shoplifters. They had learned to go for compact items, like blocks of cheese or small jars of peanut butter, things without crinkly packaging to attract attention, things they could easily slide into their waistbands or stick in their pockets. They learned how to look in one direction while reaching out to snatch something in another. When they piled back in the car after a successful "game," Shoshanna felt a confusing mixture of relief, elation, and shame. Mara was too young to feel conflicted; she was just happy to get something to eat.

"I know, I know, Shoshie," Ella said. "I don't like ripping off people any better than you do. I just don't know how else to do this. It's either that or beg for handouts. That's worse."

Shoshanna had to agree—that *was* worse. They had also done that when they lived in San Francisco. She remembered the look that came over people's faces, the way their eyes went from warm and friendly when they first saw Ella, a pretty young woman with golden-brown hair, sitting on the sidewalk with her daughter, visibly pregnant and rubbing her belly, a look that faded quickly to uncomfortable or, worse still, disgusted when they saw the handmade sign, *Broke and Hungry, Mouths to Feed*, and the paper cup outstretched in their direction. Shoshanna knew that she and the mound that would one day be her sister were props to boost her panhandling business. She hated it.

"Just this once, Shoshie, if you can grab us some food, just enough to tide us over until I can get us someplace safe where we can crash for a couple of days. After that, after we drive south, I can settle us down somewhere and find a job or sell some of my jewelry."

Shoshanna took a deep breath. If that was what it took to keep them safe… "Okay, Ma."

They drove down the road toward the highway. The little red needle that told them how much gas they had was really close to the *E* that stood for empty. A ramshackle Esso gas station appeared on their right. "Look, Ma. Gas."

They pulled in and the attendant, a pimply teenager with lank, greasy hair that kept flopping into his eyes, loped over to ask what they wanted. "Ten dollars worth of regular," Ella told him. "Do you have a restroom?"

"Yeah. Hang on. I got to give you the key. We have to keep it locked. Hippies and bums are always trying to sleep in it." He looked at her, his cheeks suddenly reddening. "No offense." He started the pump and went back inside to get the key, which he handed over without a trace of a smile. "Clean the sink off after you use it."

"We will. Come on, girls." They followed Ella to the back of the building. The bathroom was small and, considering the dejected state of the gas station, surprisingly clean. "Okay, after you pee, wash your hands and faces, and take a good, long drink of water from the sink. It's gonna have to last you."

Shoshanna enthusiastically lathered up her hands and face, and rinsed them off. Then she ducked her head under the faucet and took great gulps of cool water. The stiff paper towel was scratchy on her face, but it felt good. Mara stuck her whole head under the running water, soaking her hair and her T-shirt. When she emerged, she shook herself off like a dog. Ella laughed.

"Feels better, huh?" Ella asked.

Mara nodded, wringing out the bottom of her shirt.

"I'd feel even better if I had some food," Shoshanna said, glancing at her red and shiny face in the tiny mirror over the sink. "Seriously, Mom. My stomach is so empty it hurts."

"I know, babe." Ella mopped up the excess water and soap on the sink and flushed the toilet twice for good measure. "Let's go check out the vending machines, then." Under a red plastic awning at the front of the station, there were three machines—one for cigarettes, one for candy, and one for soda. "I would kill for a pack of Marlboros," sighed Ella. Mara began to whine in protest. "Don't worry. I'm not going to buy them. What do you guys want? We have thirty-six cents here."

"Forty-one," corrected Shoshanna.

"If the machine takes the nickel."

They decided on a box of M&M's because it would be easy to split. "We still have eleven cents left," Shoshanna announced. "Or sixteen if we're lucky."

"Gum or Life Savers are fifteen."

"Let's try the nickel, see what happens," Ella said. "Okay? How about the Life Savers?"

"Sure." Shoshanna would have preferred the gum, but she was almost sure the nickel wouldn't work.

"If the nickel works, that's a sign from the universe. It means we'll have a good day," Ella said. "Our fate hangs in the balance." They held their breath as Mara slid the nickel in the slot, added a dime, and bang, the Life Savers dropped into the tray at the bottom. Mara pushed open the plastic panel and retrieved them hastily, as if she thought someone might rush over and confiscate them.

"All right!" Ella crowed. "A good day it is."

They returned to the car, where the teenage attendant was halfheartedly washing the windshield. "You got a lot of dead bugs," he observed.

"Yeah. We've been on the road awhile. Hey, do you know how far we are from California?"

"California?" The boy laughed. "Lady, you're in it. Welcome to Eureka."

CHAPTER TWO

They found the highway again. Mara had piled all her allotted M&M's into her mouth at once, chewed them with open-mouthed gusto, and swallowed them down. Ella ate hers pretty much the same way, minus the exaggerated moans of bliss. Shoshanna cradled her M&M's in her hand, placing them one by one into her mouth. She would suck on each one until the candy shell dissolved and then allow the chocolate to melt in her mouth. They had been traveling for over an hour before she finished them, licking her palm for every vestige of chocolate for good measure.

"I wonder what they're all doing at Sweet Earth Farm right about now," Ella said. "Do you think they're freaking out?" They had been driving for a long time with the windows rolled down and the radio on. Jefferson Airplane was playing "Somebody to Love."

"I think they've been freaking out since last night. That's probably when it hit them that we're not coming back," Shoshanna replied. "They're probably over it. I bet they're getting stoned and fighting over who's gonna get our mattress."

"I bet Adam is really mad," Mara said. "I bet he wants to kill us."

"Don't say that," Shoshanna said, though she suspected her sister might be right.

Ella changed the subject. "I love this song. This station, KPFA, is in San Francisco. That's where we're headed, babies. First stop. Then we're going south." She sang along with Grace Slick. *Don't you want somebody to love? Don't you need somebody to love...*

"I don't remember much about San Francisco," said Shoshanna. "I know I was nine, but it feels like that was so long ago. It was noisy. I remember I had Snoopy sheets. I think my bed was on the floor but I could still see out the window."

Ella laughed. "Yeah. That was no window, Shosh. That was the back door. It was the only place to put your mattress." She shook her head. "That pad was wild. There must have been, like, ten people plus us crashing there and only, like, two bedrooms."

"I remember the night those guys Adam knew came

over for the money he owed them. The night we left."

"Man, oh man." Ella's fingers tapped the rim of the steering wheel. "I'm so sorry you had to see that. Talk about a bad trip. Adam was in over his head."

The trees flying by blurred and Shoshanna drifted, remembered startling awake at the banging on the door and the sharp crack of splintering wood, the angry shouts. She'd crawled out from her burrow of blankets and wandered into the harsh light of the living room to see what was going on. That's when she saw the man standing over her father, holding a gun pointed at the back of Adam's head.

Ella pushed her back into the bedroom and made her and Mara lie down on the floor underneath Mara's crib, hissing at her to *shut up, shut up*. She lay there, barely daring to breathe, staring at a pile of dust and clumps of hair and the lone raisin that had rolled under the dresser. Ella left the room even though Shoshanna, with snot running down her nose, begged her not to. The voices from the other room rose and fell. Something broke. A lamp? She heard Ella sobbing, pleading. "I promise," she heard Adam say, and some other stuff, his voice too low for her to hear what he was promising.

The door slammed, and Ella came back in and started throwing clothes into the laundry basket and, when that was full, paper bags. She remembered Adam carrying Mara to their van, and then they were on their way to Oregon. She remembered asking Adam what had happened, why they had to leave, touching his shoulder as he drove. She remembered him telling her to shut up before he elbowed her in the face. She remembered that her eye stayed swollen shut for days.

She remembered Ella promised her things would be better there, in Oregon.

"Ma, are we almost there?" Mara's voice jolted Shoshanna out of her thoughts. "I have to pee again. I'm hungry too."

"I think we're almost there. I know you're hungry, baby. We all are. The next store we come to, we'll stop. And then…you guys know what we have to do."

"How can it work without Adam?" Shoshanna asked. "Don't we need him to pull it off?"

Ella shook her head. "No. Mara and I will stay together and attract attention. Just try to pack in as much stuff as you can. Wear my work shirt, okay? Here. Keep the sleeves rolled down. Your overalls will work great, with those deep pockets."

Frowning slightly, Shoshanna put the shirt on her lap and looked out the window. Her palms began to sweat. "I hate doing this," she whispered through gritted teeth.

Ella looked at Shoshanna's grim face in the rearview mirror. "God damn. I'm sorry, Shosh. I know you hate this. This is the last time, or one of the last times, honest to God. I don't want to live like this either. When we get settled, I'll get a job. I can sell my jewelry. We can get some bread together and find a place and live like normal people." She sighed. "Okay? Oh, look. There's a store. I'm pulling in. Shosh, see if you can score some Marlboros this time, okay?" *Are you kidding?* Shoshanna thought, and just kept staring straight ahead.

The store was old and dingy. There were four towering, cramped aisles and a freezer case at the back. The cash register was at the front, which was the ideal layout for a game of family fun. Ella and Mara walked back toward the freezer and began to talk in loud voices about the ice cream selection while Shoshanna set to work. The owner, an old man with a lumpy growth that looked like a red potato sticking out of his neck, sat behind the counter, reading the newspaper though a magnifying glass. He barely bothered to look up. Shoshanna grabbed packages, fingers flying. Peanut butter, soup, a small box of crackers. Raisins, marshmallows, chocolate chip cookies. That was all she could manage, as Ella and Mara's fake argument rose in volume.

"We are *not* getting Popsicles unless you behave. I just

wanted to show you what you were missing. If you can quit whining for the next hour, until we get to Grandma's, then I'll buy you a treat." Shoshanna snatched several packets of Kool-Aid before Ella approached the store owner, who was still engrossed in his newspaper. "Excuse me, but do you have a restroom we could use?"

"Yeah, but are you buying something? The bathroom is for paying customers only."

Ella leaned over the counter, golden brown hair spilling onto the glass case, her green eyes earnest. "I'm on my way to see my parents." She beckoned for the man to come closer, lowering her voice to a breathy whisper. "I had to leave my husband, get my girls out of there fast, if you know what I mean, so I didn't have a chance to get any bread. Left my purse right on the kitchen counter and ran out."

"Well, then, don't worry about it. Here's the key. It's right out back."

Following Ella out, Shoshanna went to the car to unload her haul, then joined them in the bathroom. When they returned the key, the man was waiting with two Popsicles and a package of cupcakes. "Here you go, girls. Enjoy."

Mara's face lit up. "Thank you, mister!" *How can she not feel guilty?* Shoshanna wondered.

"Thank you," Shoshanna murmured. She couldn't bring herself to look the man in the face.

Ella returned the key. "Thank you so much," she told the man. "You've made my daughters very happy."

Back in the car, Ella looked through the food Shoshanna had thrown into the front seat. "No cigarettes?" she asked, disappointed.

"God, Ma. Sorry," Shoshanna said and turned away. "Maybe you should just be grateful for what I got."

They stopped at a rest stop right alongside the highway, and Ella made a big show of pulling out the crackers, peanut butter, and raisins. "I didn't mean to put you down about not getting the cigarettes. I know that wasn't cool. You did a good job, Shosh. We're gonna need some water for the Kool-Aid, though."

Using their index fingers, they spread the peanut butter thickly on top of the crackers, which they then studded with raisins. They washed their feast down with cool water from the water fountain. For the first time in days, Shoshanna and Mara felt as if they'd had enough to eat.

"Can I have a marshmallow for dessert?" Mara asked, licking a stray blob of peanut butter from her thumb.

"We should save the rest of the food for later when we're hungry again," Ella said, brushing the crumbs off the picnic table. She stood up, taking the empty cracker box and tossing it into a trash can. "Shosh, grab the raisins.

Mara, close up that peanut butter. There's a port-a-potty over there. Why don't you both go for one last pee? Then we should get back on the road. I looked at the map on the wall in the restroom, and if I read it right, I am pretty sure we can make it to San Francisco before dark."

When they got back on the road, Mara sprawled belly-down on the length of the backseat, and Shoshanna sat up front with Ella, knees tucked against her chest. The sun kept breaking free of the clouds, then retreating behind them. Shoshanna began to doze, watching the pattern of light that appeared and disappeared on the dashboard through half-shut eyes. She wished she could stop thinking about Adam. She imagined him following close behind in the farm truck. She imagined him holding the shotgun he'd used to kill the litter of unwanted puppies that time, or the knife he'd held to Ella's throat when she wouldn't leave their mattress to go back with him to his room with Melaya.

The sound of Mara snoring softly in the backseat brought her back to the present. Her mother spoke. "Man, look at that. We're low on gas again. We'll just have to get as far as we can and hustle some bread. Just for gas, Shosh. Just to get us there. Then I'm going to get a job."

Would things ever change? Shoshanna stared out the window as miles of silver guardrail flew by. A job. She'd believe that when she saw it. But then, up until yesterday, she would never have believed that they would get out of Sweet Earth, much less all the way to California. A ladybug crawled up the window. Was it inside the car or out? She tapped on the glass. Outside. How could a little bug like that hang on, rattling forty-five miles an hour down the highway? Were ladybugs supposed to be lucky or something? Maybe it was a good omen, like the Life Savers. Or maybe Life Savers were just candy, and the ladybug was just some dumb bug that knew how to stick on a window.

She opened her eyes when Ella touched her shoulder. They were driving over an orange bridge. She could see the thick cables towering above and the water and dramatically craggy green hills alongside. "Wow."

"Here we are, the Golden Gate Bridge. Isn't it cool? We made it. San Fran was closer than I thought."

"It's not golden. It's orange. Why do they call it golden?"

"Beats me." Ella shrugged, then let out a small whoop of joy. "San Francisco. Home of Rice-A-Roni, the San Francisco treat. Rice-A-Roni, the flavor can't be beat." It hasn't changed."

"Rice a what?"

"Never mind. That's just a stupid TV commercial jingle."

Mara's head perked up. "TV! Can we get one?"

"Jesus, Mar. One thing at a time, okay?" Ella's enthusiasm faded swiftly into weary annoyance. "First we have to find a place to stay."

Ella eased the station wagon, which had recently developed an ominous-sounding tinny rattle, off the highway and onto city streets. With every bump, every pothole, the ancient shocks squeaked and groaned. "This car sounds like it's on its last legs."

"Tires," Shoshanna corrected, watching out the window as a bum walked up to a man in a business suit standing at the corner, briefcase in hand, poised to cross. The bum put out his hand and said something. He must've been asking for money, Shoshanna figured, like they used to do. Like they might have to do now. The man shook his head, stepped to the side, and crossed the street. She watched as the bum raised his middle finger to the man's retreating back.

"Where are we, Ma? Is this where we used to live?"

"No. Man, living down here would have been a total bummer. I don't even know how I got here. I must've missed my exit. This is the Mission. Look around, Shoshie, it's nothing but lowlifes, winos, and hookers. We lived in a place called Haight-Ashbury. The Haight's a real funky neighborhood on the other side of town, closer to the park."

"I remember the park, Mom." Shoshanna had a sudden, very vivid memory of lying on a blanket and squinting up at the sun sifting gold through the leaves of the trees while someone strummed on a guitar. That was a good memory. Adam wasn't in it.

"Golden Gate Park. We used to go there a lot. All us hippies used to hang out there. It was fun, like a party that never stopped."

Shoshanna dimly remembered something else not so pleasant: running through the grass barefoot and stepping on a smoldering cigarette. At first everyone thought she'd been stung by a bee. It left a small scar shaped like a crescent moon on the instep of her right foot.

It was like Ella read her mind and linked Shoshanna's memory to her own current fixation: "God, I would give my right arm for a smoke." Ella's fingers continued their habitual nervous tapping on the steering wheel. She bit her lower lip and frowned. "Damn. I'm *dying*. Anyway, if we get over to the Haight, we can visit our old pad and see who still lives there. Maybe we'll get lucky and whoever it is will remember us or even just take pity on us and let us crash for the night."

The station wagon rattled and shuddered up an impossibly steep hill. Shoshanna was genuinely afraid that the car wasn't going to make it and they would go hurtling backward over the cable car tracks and intersections before smashing into some building. In Oregon, they were surrounded by mountains, but Sweet Earth was nestled in the shelter of a deep valley. Here in San Francisco, every hill seemed to be covered with row upon row of narrow houses stacked side by side.

Mara looked out the window, eyes wide, hair a mass of tangles and static electricity. She slid back down and tugged at her sister's arm. "I don't like this place," she whispered.

"We just got here. How do you even know if you like it or not? Anyway, it's not like we're going to stay."

"I heard that, Mara baby. Give San Fran a chance. It's a groovy city, or at least it used to be. Hey, look. This is where the Haight begins. Man. Okay, that's the Lucky grocery where we used to buy our groceries. And that's the Psychedelic Shop. I sold them stuff, macramé mostly, some beaded stuff. I was just getting into jewelry then. I didn't really know what I was doing but they were cool. They bought my stuff anyway. Probably because they felt sorry for me, being pregnant out to here"—she indicated some point past the steering wheel—"with Mara. I looked like a grasshopper that swallowed an elephant." Mara giggled.

The houses in the Haight were typical of most neighborhoods in San Francisco—narrow Victorians, three stories high, stacked alongside each other. This neighborhood was better than the Mission but not as nice as the ones they'd driven through to get to it, Shoshanna thought, though she didn't tell Ella that. She never wanted to be the bummer when Ella was in one of her good moods.

Some of the windows were boarded up, paint was peeling, and weeds grew tall in many front yards. "Make Love, Not War" was spray-painted against a brick building in blood-red letters. A man and a woman stood on a street corner, locked together and swaying. It looked like they would both fall down if either one let go.

"There it is, 65 Clayton Street. Man, would you look at that," Ella murmured, shaking her head. She slowed the car down and looked over at a narrow brown-and-beige Victorian with a gingerbread-trimmed turret. The first floor was boarded up, but the second and third floors seemed to be occupied. At least, there were lace curtains on some of the windows, and it looked like a light or candle was burning. "Hang on. We'll park and see who lives here."

"It looks scary, Mom. Like there was a fire or something." The boarded-up first floor made the house look bleak and forbidding.

"Yeah. We lived on the first floor, Shosh, d'you remember? I wonder what happened, why it's boarded up. Maybe you're right about a fire. The trim around the door and windows looks charred. But someone's living upstairs." Ella parked the car and turned to her daughters. "Okay. Let's go. The side door isn't boarded up. That must be the way in."

"But what if it's some weird person living up there, Mom? That would be so embarrassing."

"Why? We'll just tell them we used to live here and we were curious to see how the place looks. Ask if there was a fire. No big deal, Shosh. Come on."

Shoshanna followed reluctantly; it wasn't like she had a choice. They emerged from the car, stiff and more than a little bit disoriented, and followed Ella up the uneven sidewalk to the front door. Mara reached for Shoshanna's hand, and Shoshie held it, even though it was still sticky from the M&M's. She felt weary, hopeless. Things never changed. Her mother was big on promises, on getting someplace better, on things being different. Forget the sunshine and orange trees. Instead, they would probably be breaking into an abandoned house.

Ella took a deep breath and rang the bell. There was no sound. She tried again. "I guess it's broken." She knocked on the wooden door, at first quietly, then with gusto. They heard the sound of approaching footsteps coming down the stairs.

"Hang on, I'm coming," said a woman's voice. The heavy wooden door swung open, and behind it stood a tall young woman with blond hair down to her waist, high cheekbones, and sparkling hazel eyes, wearing a pair of patched, faded jeans and scuffed leather sandals. *She doesn't look that much older than me*, Shoshanna thought. Maybe twenty-two or twenty-three, she guessed. She was pretty, even with the look of exasperation on her face that slowly turned to a wide, incredulous grin. "No way. No way! Shit! Is that *you*? Ella?"

"Judy!" Ella screamed. "Far out! I can't believe you're still here."

"My God, I never thought I'd see you again! Man. Look at you." She pulled Ella inside and hugged her tight. "You look good. Good but tired, Mama. Tired and worn out. And skinny. Don't they feed you at that crazy-ass commune?"

"Yeah." Ella smiled. "But not well and not often." For the first time, Shoshanna noticed the circles under her mother's eyes and the way her bony shoulders sagged forward as if she was always saddled with a heavy burden. "I left Adam."

"High time. What a piece-of-crap scumbag. Damn, sorry, El. I didn't see the kids. Though you're hardly a kid," she said, looking at Shoshanna. "You must be Shoshie and, um, I forget your name, little one."

"Mara."

"Right. You were so tiny when you left. How old are you now?"

"Five," Mara said. "Almost six. Shoshie's fourteen."

"Almost fifteen," said Shoshanna. Shoshanna looked over Judy's shoulder and up the stairs toward the apartment. The door to the apartment was open and she could smell something wonderful baking—cake, maybe, or bread. She couldn't help it; her mouth started watering. She found herself hoping beyond hope that Judy would invite them to stay for dinner.

Judy shook her head. "Man, where does the time go? Do you remember this place at all, Shoshanna?"

Shoshanna shrugged. "Yeah. Some stuff. I remember there were other people living with us. People were always playing music. And you had to wait your turn for the bathroom."

"This was a cool place to live back then. The fun was just getting started. You guys left before the Summer of Love. That was so groovy, El, so many cool people, so many good vibes. Then everything started to turn. It's not a good scene now. Everywhere you look, it's bad trips and burnouts. I mean, look at your old place downstairs."

"What happened?" Ella asked.

"There was a fire, lots of smoke and water damage, but the landlord was trying to fix it when people kept breaking in and ripping off whatever stuff they could find in there. He got tired of kicking out the junkies trying to crash there, so he boarded it up. I don't even blame him. It used to be so free and easy here. Not anymore." Judy paused to survey the three of them, taking in their dirty faces and unkempt hair. "It looks like you haven't been having an easy time either."

"It's a long story." Ella shook her head. "You were right about Adam."

"We were all right about Adam, El. You were so in love with him that you were blind to what he was all about. I mean, he was a charismatic dude. Good-looking too. Shoshie, you look like him. Same beautiful brown eyes."

"Thanks," Shoshie said, though she didn't know quite how to feel about this observation, which people made all the time. She knew she had her father's coloring, his straight nose, his chestnut brown hair and dark eyes, his long, skinny legs, his full lips. This was a compliment, she knew, but she hated the fact she resembled him in any way, because she worried she might have inherited not just his looks, but his nature. Sometimes when she looked into a mirror, she saw him, and for a moment, she couldn't breathe.

"That's meant to be a compliment. Adam is a handsome devil. Emphasis on the devil." Judy grinned and put her hands on Shoshanna and Mara's shoulders. "Man, you are two scrawny little chicks. So much for healthy life on the commune. What's it called? I know your mom told me, but I forgot."

"Sweet Earth Farm," Shoshanna replied.

"Sweet Earth. What a crock of shit," Judy said, shaking her head. "I'm sorry. I should warn you guys that I have a terrible habit of saying exactly what's on my mind."

Shoshie smiled. "I think I figured that out. And actually, I don't mind. I like hearing the truth."

Judy looked at Shoshie and nodded her head. "I have a feeling we're going to get along really well, Shosh. Come on inside, girlies. Auntie Judy will take care of you. Lucky for you I just put some bread in the oven." They piled into the hallway. Shoshanna felt lighter just hearing those words. To stop running, to have someone taking care of them for once—the gratitude she felt was almost overwhelming.

"Will you take care of me too?" Ella whispered to Judy.

"Baby, you know I will. Crash here. I'm on my own these days too. Erik split around two months ago. He's in L.A. with some stupid blond teenybopper who's the same age as I was when he managed to win me over with his trademark brand of bullshit. I think he has her convinced he can make her a movie star. Like he has the ability to do anything other than hustle suckers out of their pot money." They walked through a narrow hall and up a flight of stairs. Along with the smell of the bread, Shoshanna noticed the faint lingering smell of the charred wood leaching up from the first floor.

When they got to the top of the stairs and entered Judy's apartment, the charred smell vanished. Inside was purely magical. Mara and Shoshanna gasped in delight at the throw pillows scattered on the hot-pink painted floor and the walls decorated with Day-Glo posters of flowers. Every wall was painted a different vivid color— purple, turquoise, bright yellow, deep green. An ancient sofa, with springs sagging to the floor, was covered with maroon-and-gold Indian-print fabric in a pattern almost identical to Ella's skirt. A calico cat lay big bellied and motionless on the window ledge.

"Don't mind the cat; it's just a neighborhood stray. I call him Desperado. He comes in through the window and begs for food, which I give him. I think he knows a pushover when he sees one. How about some tea to go along with your bread?"

"I'd love tea. Water's fine for the girls."

"Do you have any chocolate milk?" asked Mara.

"No, babe, sorry." Judy smiled. "Just tea and water. I can run down to the corner store and get you some."

"Water will be fine, Jude. Quit asking for stuff, okay,

Mara? You're such a mooch. Jeez."

"Don't worry about it. Listen, I want to give you guys anything you want."

They sat down, Mara and Shoshanna on the couch, Ella in an old wooden chair, while Judy sat cross-legged on the floor. "This a great pad," Ella said.

"Yeah. I can keep it a lot neater without strangers crashing and trashing it every night like in the old days. And it was crazy. When people began moving out, they left all kinds of cool shit behind. I just acquired most of this stuff."

"It's so quiet here, Judy. Where's your kid?"

"What kid?"

"Weren't you, like, seven or eight months pregnant when we took off? *That* kid."

"Yeah, right. Right. God, I forgot that happened after you left."

"What? What happened?"

Judy looked at a patch of sunlight on the floor and blinked her eyes. When she raised her head, she looked at Ella for a moment, then rested her gaze on the sleeping cat. Her voice was quiet. "The baby—it was a boy. He was stillborn. The placenta tore, and at first they didn't know why. It was awful. One day he was kicking like crazy, and then he just stopped and I started bleeding. I knew it the second he died. It was like someone blowing out a candle. His soul was, poof, gone.

"We named him Che, after Che Guevara. I had to go through labor anyway. I just screamed the whole time. Then they found this fibroid tumor thing, which was why the placenta detached, so they put me under and took everything out. Total hysterectomy. Scooped me clean. Here I am, twenty-three, and I can't ever have kids."

"God, Jude, I'm sorry…"

Hearing Judy's story made Shoshanna feel a little sick to her stomach. Not so much because of the sad details but because Shoshanna could tell Judy obviously wanted to be a mother. It was not something Shoshanna had any personal experience with. She remembered that Ella was not happy when she found out she was pregnant with Mara. She remembered her crying, telling Adam that she was afraid the acid would mess the baby up. She remembered Adam laughing at her and telling everyone that the baby probably wasn't his, anyway.

That was when Ella threatened to leave, and Adam moved out of their house and in with another woman, Indigo, who read tarot cards and once told Shoshanna that she could see the black spot in her heart. She remembered Ella screaming when she gave birth to Mara, and blood all over the place. Adam's first words after seeing Mara's blond hair and blue eyes were, "I told you. The kid's not mine."

✳ ✳ ✳

Shoshanna shook her head, trying to clear the dark thoughts from it, and inhaled deeply, returning gratefully to the present and savoring the scent of Judy's apartment, of baked bread and something else spicy and sweet. "It smells so good in here."

"Thanks. It's a blend I'm working on—sandalwood, musk, and patchouli. I'm trying to get into scented oils as a business sideline. I'm staying open to different sensory and retail experiences. The posters are selling for now, but who knows how long that's going to last? I mean, psychedelics and Peter Max were big last year, and now no one's into that kind of stuff. Right now I'm digging hand-painting old photographs."

She showed them a stack of old black-and-white photographs that she had tinted with watercolors. The landscapes were tinted delicate greens and browns, and the portraits, mostly of women or children, had delicate pink tint added to cheeks and lips, and blue or green added to the eyes.

"Cool, huh? It's actually a very old process. It's what they used to do to color photographs before Kodachrome came out. I'm selling tons of these to card shops at, like, two bucks apiece."

Shoshanna couldn't get over how Judy was so resilient—the opposite of her mother, who kept letting every obstacle she came upon cause her to skitter away or stop cold. Maybe some of Judy's spirit would rub off on Ella. That would be something to hope for.

Ella took a sip of the tea and began to cough.

"Are you okay?" Judy asked. "Do you need water?"

"No, I'm fine. It's just a little hot, and it went down the wrong way."

Judy disappeared for a minute into the cluttered galley kitchen, and Shoshanna leaned over and peered in to see a bright room with narrow counters covered with mysterious substances in jars and old plastic cottage-cheese containers. There was yogurt culturing, extravagantly fermenting yeast, soybeans and alfalfa layered and covered with damp cheesecloth to encourage sprouting. Judy emerged with a loaf of whole grain bread, thickly sliced, with a plume of steam still rising from it. Along with the bread was a tray with honey and sesame tahini and homemade peanut butter. The girls set upon the still-warm loaf like starving pups.

"Whoa! Man! When was the last time you guys ate?" Judy asked.

"Do you mean counting what Shoshie stoled from the store, or real food that we bought?" asked Mara.

Judy looked quizzically at Ella. Ella shrugged. Judy shook her head. "God. Um, real food, I guess."

"Two days ago." Shoshanna dripped so much honey on her bread that it began to seep through. She used a second slice to sop it up. "We tried to leave with some food, but it was too risky. We had to save our money for gas."

"Things must not be going too well at Sweet Earth," Judy murmured.

"Yeah," Ella said. "Yeah. But we're out now."

"I hate to bring this up, but what would you have done if I didn't still live here?"

"I don't know." Ella stroked Mara's head. "Live in the car for a while, I guess. Panhandle. Maybe try to look up some old friends."

"You'd be shit out of luck on that one," Judy said, pouring herself some more tea. "They pretty much all split. In fact, I've been thinking, like seriously thinking, about leaving too. I mean, there's nothing going on here, outside of the junkies and the tourists coming to stand on the corner of Haight and Ashbury taking pictures like we're in some psychedelic freak show. Plus, there's like a porn shop on every corner. It's not like it used to be. It's got a whole different vibe, you know, and not a good vibe, real negative. I was thinking of leaving for a few months but I couldn't get my act together. Maybe this is fate, and I was supposed to wait for you. You were always big on fate, Ella."

"Maybe this is fate. But these days I find I'm equally big on just random stuff happening for no reason. The how and the why doesn't even really matter, Jude. All that matters is you're still here." Ella walked over to the window and looked out. "Crazy. It looks like there are more tourists than hippies."

"Yeah. Like I said, things have turned."

"Where were you thinking of going?"

"Well, I met this couple at a Joplin concert at the Fillmore last year. The guy, his name's Jim, used to be, like, a philosophy professor or something at Berkeley, and then he started tripping on acid a few times a week and he quit, or maybe he got fired. Who knows. The woman he's with—she may be his wife or maybe not—she's this gorgeous Asian woman named Francine. They're super cool, very laid back. Anyway, they were running this shop in the Haight, right near the Panhandle. You know, on that corner where the Russian guy had that crazy Laundromat that ate all our change, remember? Adam totally kicked his ass, and that was one time I was happy to see him lose his cool.

"Anyhow, I used to sell posters to their shop, and when I was into erotic candle making—that's a whole other story; I'll have to tell you that one after the kids have gone to bed—they bought some of those too, like on consignment. But anyway, the cops busted them because they were selling pot in the back room. I mean, big deal, right? Everyone and his uncle was selling grass, and the cops shoulda been more worried about the heroin and crystal dealers.

"Anyhow, Jim and Francine were sick of getting hassled, so they moved down to Half Moon Bay. It's twenty miles south of here, down the peninsula, north of San Jose. It's right by the ocean and it's supposed to be cool. There's a redwood forest and lots of hills but some artichoke and pumpkin farms, and it has its share of displaced hippies. I saw Jim and Francine in the park last week, and they told me I should come visit. That made me start thinking about moving out of the Haight permanently. Jim said they get people hitting the beaches on the weekends and you can do okay with crafts. The pigs leave you alone down there too."

"I'd be into that." Ella smiled, and for the first time since Shoshanna could remember, she saw a light come into her mother's eyes. "Did I tell you I've been making jewelry?"

"Yeah?"

"Uh-huh. Cool stuff. Here, I'll show you. Shosh, could you throw me my bag? It's next to that lamp there."

Shoshanna, her belly full to the point of genuine discomfort, stood up slowly. She could actually hear the contents of her stomach sloshing around. She handed over her mother's bag, a striped, coarse wool sack with a llama design on it and plenty of fringe, the Peruvian spoils of a flea-market barter. Ella rummaged around and pulled out a plastic bag that held a few of her favorite pieces.

"These are totally happening," said Judy, turning the bracelets and rings over in her fingers. "I especially love these rings. How did you make the bands?"

"Just take a closer look and I bet you can figure it out." Judy did, and shook her head. "They're old sterling-silver spoon handles. Isn't that a trip?"

"How'd you get old sterling-silver spoons?"

Ella looked away. "Adam. I don't ask questions. Anyway, I just heated them up and molded them into shape, then reheated the silver to set the stones."

"That's wild."

"Yeah, I sold probably fifty to shops in Portland and Corvallis. The bracelets do really well too. See the spoon handle on them? I can get ten bucks apiece wholesale, and I bet they turn around and sell them for double or even triple. Some of the guys from Sweet Earth would take a bunch of stuff to the flea market along with the apples, but no one at the flea market ever had cash. They always try to barter, and I'd feel kind of gypped when Adam came home with six cartons of cigarettes and a used water pipe for ten of my best bracelets." Ella shook her head. "Anyway, I have some stuff with me, stones and silver and stuff, and my little baby blowtorch. Lucky for me no one took it out of the wagon before we split."

"Cool." Judy got up to carry the empty tray back to the kitchen. "I have a great idea, seeing that you have a car."

"We have Sweet Earth's wagon, yeah."

Judy looked alarmed. "Wait. You think they followed you? Or called the cops?"

Ella shook her head. "I don't think so."

"Think? I don't feel good about this, El. We can't risk Adam coming down here. I don't need to tell you what he'd do to you. To me. To the girls. We have to take your stuff out of the car and move it somewhere no one will see it." For the first time since the girls arrived, Judy sounded worried. "Then we'll drive down to Half Moon Bay tomorrow. No one's going to look for you there. I mean, it's a small town. I'm sure we can find Jim and Francine if we ask around. They're probably pretty conspicuous. I'll bring my posters and cards, you bring your jewelry, and we'll see what happens."

"That sounds great. Hey, girls, help Judy with the dishes, okay? I'll get the stuff out of the car."

"Never mind the dishes, girls. You go help your mother. I can take care of this."

"Judy is the best," Mara told Shoshanna as they climbed the stairs back to her apartment.

Shoshanna hated to allow herself, or encourage Mara, to trust that anything could be legitimately good these days, but she could only agree that yes, Judy was the best. Coming here was the best. She felt like a marathon swimmer who'd finally made it to shore safely. If you'd told her yesterday this was where they'd wind up, welcomed with open arms into this cozy, soft nest, she would never have believed it.

That night, Shoshanna and Mara lay side by side in Judy's big brass bed. Judy and Ella were going to sleep on the couch in the living room so they could stay up and talk. The girls bounced on the mattress and ducked under the clean white sheets. "I love it here," said Mara. "That was the best dinner in the whole world."

"Yeah," said Shoshanna. "Chicken and rice and green beans and strawberries. And there was enough for all of us."

"Do you think maybe we can stay here forever?"

"Maybe," Shoshanna said, even though she knew that wasn't the Plan, and that the Plan was always shifting.

Mara snuggled into the mattress, sighed happily, then turned over to face the wall. Right under the flower poster that proclaimed "War is Not Healthy for Children and Other Living Things" was a hole in the plaster the size of a fist.

"I bet someone got mad."

"Yeah," Shoshanna said. "But I bet that was a long time ago." Shoshie squeezed her eyes shut and opened them, testing the magic she wanted to possess as a kid, being able to use her mind to make ugly things disappear. When she looked again, the hole was still there.

Mara's breathing deepened. Shoshanna turned over the thoughts in her head. It worried her, what Judy said to Ella about Adam. *I don't need to tell you what he'd do to you.* Shoshanna knew too. Last year, there was the hitchhiker who somehow found his way to Sweet Earth, stayed for dinner, dropped some acid, and after a bad trip, sweating, screaming, twitching, he died right there, right before her eyes. She couldn't get it out of her head, the way he was thrashing around on the floor, banging his head against the wall.

She couldn't forget the way Adam looked at the boy's skinny, limp body, eyes rolled back in his head, hands contorted like bird claws, and just shrugged, like it was nothing more than a small inconvenience before grabbing a couple of Sweet Earthers to help him throw the boy's body into the river. She remembered them checking his jeans pockets to see if he had any money. (He didn't.) And Ella had just stood there, her face blank. She said nothing. Shoshanna was crying *Help him, help him*, and all Ella did was stand there, picking at a scab on her arm like nothing was happening. Like this boy was…disposable.

Shoshanna kicked up from the murky bottom of her memory, carrying her thoughts to the light at the surface. This was her life in this moment—a soft bed, a little sister who sometimes felt like a yoke around her neck but who she loved with all her heart, and the unfamiliar sound of her mother's laughter bubbling in from the kitchen. She felt safe. Turning away from the hole in the wall, she slept.

CHAPTER THREE

Shoshanna woke up. Everything was unfamiliar, disorienting. Then, she remembered where she was and felt a surge of happiness. She climbed over Mara, who was still fast asleep, hair coiled around her grubby fingers. Gray fog blanketed the street, softening the corners of buildings and dampening the sounds of the passing cars. She could hear drawers opening and plates rattling in the kitchen. It was a good sound, a sound of industry tinged with anticipation.

At Sweet Earth Farm, the rooster crowed early, and whoever had the job of cleaning out the chicken coop and gathering eggs could be heard shuffling up the path, usually swearing to himself or herself. Otherwise, though, dawn was silent. It wasn't like anyone had any place to be at any particular time. People got up when they got up, and depending upon what had gone on the night before, people generally got up late. Some days, Adam didn't get up at all, and some days when Ella was down, she only got out of bed when the girls forced her out.

"Come on, Mara. We're in San Francisco. Time to get up." Shoshanna felt it was urgent for them to savor this day. She didn't want to waste a second sleeping.

Mara moaned. "Let me sleep, Shoshie. I'm so *comferble*."

"We'll have plenty of time to sleep later. Come on." Shoshanna pulled on the same clothes she'd been wearing, minus the bottom layer, which was beginning to smell. "Fine. You just lie here then and waste the whole day. I'm gonna go eat breakfast. I bet Judy has really good food." The mention of good food was generally enough to get Mara going. Mara exhaled deeply, then sat up.

"Wait for me," she said, pulling on her shirt.

Judy and Ella were in the kitchen, talking quietly. Judy moved quickly and gracefully, a domestic ballet, setting out glasses and bowls and spoons for all of them. Her long hair was brushed and braided, and she wore a faded red T-shirt and an oversized pair of men's denim overalls. Ella, with her brown hair piled on her head and still wearing her gauzy, printed skirt and peasant blouse, leaned over the counter, brows furrowed. She was studying a map.

"Hey, Shoshie. How'd you sleep?" asked Judy.

"Really good." Shoshanna said. "It's so quiet here. At home the rooster wakes us up. I hate the rooster."

"Glad to hear city life agrees with you. Do you like granola? I make my own."

"Sure. That sounds great. My mom makes her own too."

"Listen. You know what my granola secret is?" Judy asked. "Your mom's gonna hate this. Let me whisper in your ear." Obligingly, Shoshanna moved closer and tilted her head. "Chocolate."

"I heard that," Ella said, refolding the map.

Judy rolled her eyes. "Okay, okay, Miss I'd Kill for a Cigarette. Don't you think you're being just a little hypocritical? Come on, Shosh. I'm going to introduce you to the best granola you've ever had, topped with brown sugar and cinnamon and homemade yogurt and a drizzle of honey. You will swoon with delight." Placing the bowl heaped with granola in front of Shoshanna, Judy then proceeded to unleash a steady stream of pasteurized, homogenized goodness over the tantalizing mountain of grains, chocolate, raisins, yogurt, and honey.

Mara padded into the kitchen. "What are you eating, Shosh?"

"Just the most amazing granola to ever be created in the history of the world," Judy said.

"Can I have some too?" Mara asked.

"Coming right up," said Judy.

"I can't bear to stay here and watch you corrupt my kids like this with chocolate and processed sugar and pasteurized milk," Ella said. "I won't stop you because I'm a guest in your house and that wouldn't be polite, but I won't watch." She walked out the door and down the steps.

"Do you think she's really mad?" Mara asked. She was almost impossible to understand through the mouthful of cereal and milk.

"Not really," Shoshanna replied. "She's just jonesing for a cigarette and she needed an out. It's okay, Mare."

"Come on, girls, eat up. We have a big day ahead of us," Judy chimed in.

"This tastes so good," Mara said between spoonfuls. "But why is this a big day? Where are we going?"

"Your mother and I talked about things some more last night after you two went to bed, and we decided to leave the city for the day. It wouldn't be cool if your dad and the others knew where you are, after taking the car like you did, so we thought it would be a good time to take off. The plan is to visit my friends Jim and Francine today. They have a cool shop in Half Moon Bay, around thirty miles away from here, right on the water. They said a while back they would sell my posters and they might sell my cards, so I thought your mother could see if they'd sell her jewelry. Maybe after we check it out, we can come back here, pack up, and find a place to live out there until things calm down."

"That makes sense," Shoshanna said, though she wished she didn't have to get back in the car again. It was okay, though, as long as she could spend another night in Judy's bed. "I hope we can spend tomorrow here in San Francisco. It looks like so much fun."

"Maybe we can. But Half Moon Bay should be nice too," Judy told her. "And for now, the priority is keeping everyone safe. We can come back after dark."

"Is Half Moon Bay near Disneyland?" Mara asked.

Judy laughed. "No, baby. Disneyland is, like, four hundred miles away. It's down south, near Los Angeles. It's a whole different scene, a whole different part of California."

"My mom promised we could go there." Mara frowned, her voice heavy with disappointment. "That was the Plan."

"Well, if it's the Plan, I'm sure you will get there eventually, just not today. Today we'll get to go to the beach, though. It'll be fun. I promise."

Ella came back, slightly out of breath. She was carrying a paper bag full of apples. "Here's something healthy to balance the crap you've all been eating. Someone must've left these in the trunk of our station wagon. Don't let the bruises and worm holes bother you, Jude. These are totally DDT free and organic and really tasty. Just be careful where you bite."

"Thanks, El. Maybe I'll make some pie with them later. Or applesauce. That would be good." She put the bag on the counter. "Okay, then. If you get your jewelry together, I'll pack up the posters and some of the colorized cards. I think Jim and Francine will really dig them. You got the map?"

"Yeah. Not that I can read it."

"Leave that to me. Girls, get your stuff. We're going on an adventure."

Leaving the apartment, Shoshanna paused in the doorway and took everything in. She allowed the calm order of Judy's apartment, the homeyness, and the sweet smells to wash over her. She couldn't shake the feeling that, like a good dream, this wasn't meant to last.

Judy had hidden the car in an alley behind a burned-out building. "Good," she said. "It's still here. I was afraid that maybe it would get towed. It looks like abandoned junk."

"It runs," Ella said. "That's all that matters. I was thinking maybe we can paint it. Get some California plates for it. That way if Adam sent any spies out…"

"I think the smartest thing we can do is get out of Dodge for the day," Judy said.

It didn't take them long to get to Half Moon Bay. As they drove south, the morning sun began to burn through the foggy haze, and patches of blue sky emerged. They could see glimpses of the Pacific from time to time, a deep gray with glints of silver. They passed through a town on a hill covered with small ranch houses, all identical to each other except for the colors, like a child's blocks. They drove until the houses were farther apart, then gradually replaced by steep, craggy hills and ravines covered by evergreen trees before descending once again into a valley with fields and small farms.

"We're almost there," Judy said.

Ella grinned. "I can smell the ocean. I forgot how much I dig the ocean breeze. It's pretty nice out here."

"Yeah, it is. I always said I'd never leave the city. I actually made a poster that had a photograph of a country club lady and her two perfect kids that said "Death by Suburbia." It sold pretty well. But now...I don't know. This seems so tranquil, so pure. Maybe I'm getting old."

Ella laughed. "Old? Remember 'Don't trust anyone over thirty'? I can't believe I'm two years older than that." Ella suddenly looked into the rearview mirror. "Hey, you see that maroon car in back of us? They've been behind us for the last ten miles."

Shoshanna turned around. "It's a Mercedes, Ma, with

California plates. Unless Adam suddenly came into some serious cash…"

Ella relaxed. "Thanks. I don't know why I'm so paranoid."

"Well, I do, and I don't blame you," Judy said. "The sooner we can ditch this car, the better, in my opinion."

"I don't think Dad would ever hurt us," Mara piped up. "Once he gave me some sugar if I promised not to tell on him about the lady in his bed."

Shoshanna shot Mara a warning look. "Shh, Mare."

"Fine." Mara turned to look out the window. "But he did."

"Jeez, Mare…" Shoshanna shook her head.

"That's okay, Shosh. I knew. I knew about all the ladies." Ella took a cigarette from her bag. "I found someone's stash in the back of the wagon. Half a carton. Finders, keepers," she laughed.

"Ugh. I really hate cigarettes, El. It's a nasty habit. Hey, let's turn down there. It looks like the main street or something."

"I have a feeling you're right. Man, you'll never guess what it's called: Main Street."

Judy nodded and laughed. "It's sweet. Kind of like this place got stuck in a fifties time warp."

Shoshanna stared at the row of modest storefronts—a dry cleaners, a coffee shop, and a shoe repair. "Nothing personal, but I liked San Francisco way better. Half Moon Bay looks boring. Kind of like Grants Pass."

"I liked your apartment," Mara chimed in. "Yesterday was the best day in the world."

Judy turned around and looked at Mara. "For me too, baby doll. When we get back to my house tonight, I'm going to give you a bubble bath. You'll dig it. Bubbles are groovy. Then I'll tell you a story before tucking you in. You can listen too, Shosh, even though I guess you're too old for bedtime stories." Shoshanna was surprised to see Judy's eyes get watery and watched as she brushed the back of her cheek with her hand.

"That's okay. I like stories," she said, thinking how she was always the one asked to tell them to Mara. It would be wonderful to be able to relax and do the listening.

Ella let out a low whistle. "Judy, look over there. 'Jim and Francine's Co-Op Artisans' Haven.'"

"We found it! Like we were led to it! It's a sign, Ella. From the universe. It's freaking fate. Park this ark. Here, grab this space."

"I don't think that's a space. It's too close to the crosswalk."

"Come on, Ella. Since when did you become a law-abiding citizen? I bet there are, like, three cops on the force in this entire town. What do they care if your car's in a crosswalk? I'm sure they have more important things to do with their time, like eating donuts and drinking coffee."

"I hope you're right." Ella pulled the car over and they clambered out.

"It is over the line, Ma," Shoshanna said.

"Look what you've gone and done. You've made your girl a worrier, El," Judy said. "Like I told your mom, Shoshie, relax. This is a hick town. No one cares."

To anyone passing by, they made an odd foursome: Ella and her daughters looked more like destitute 1930s migrant farmworkers than hippies. Mara had run out of clean clothes and had put on one of Judy's old T-shirts that could pass for a dress. Her yellow hair was a tangled mass, and the edges of her lips were powdered with dried milk and sugar from her breakfast.

Shoshanna had put on her overalls for the third day running (it was a choice between that and a pair of patched jeans) and a striped shirt that had picked up small thorns from her last trek through the fields back in Oregon. She tied her hair back with a kerchief so it wouldn't flop in her face. She kept getting poked by embedded thorns that she had to ease out using her thumb and forefinger. Ella topped her long, printed skirt with an embroidered peasant blouse that had a sizable rip under the right armpit that revealed a thick patch of underarm hair.

Seeing Ella without a shawl or a sweater, Shoshanna was shocked to see that her mother had gotten so thin over the past year. Her bony collarbone protruded, and her hazel eyes were ringed by dark bluish-purple circles. Judy had thrown a denim work shirt on top of her overalls. *She looks healthy, strong enough to take care of anything*, Shoshanna thought. She also thought that if Mara's hair was brushed and her face was clean, she would look more like she belonged to Judy than Ella.

Then she remembered something Adam had said a few months ago. He was hugging Mara, but then he'd looked over at Shoshanna and his eyes narrowed. "You're mine, dark one. This one belongs to the sun." Adam often said crazy things when he was tripping, which she was pretty sure he was at the time, so she tried to ignore him. But somehow, as nonsensical as that comment had seemed, it stayed with her. It made her feel like she was cursed.

"Come on, girls," Judy said. "I want you to meet a couple of friends of mine."

They opened a door and a massive wind chime made of steel pipes and hollow bamboo clanged their arrival. The shop was stacked full of the most amazingly incongruous potpourri of objects. There were wooden toys, pottery, bumper stickers, posters, handmade dresses, hash pipes and rolling papers, fragments of stained-glass window, macramé plant holders, and used books. Nothing was in any logical order but the net effect was cheerful rather than cluttered. They stood there for several minutes, looking around in wonder while waiting for someone to emerge. No one did.

"Hey, Jim? Francine? It's Judy from Clayton Street. I've brought some friends down to meet you."

About a minute later, a man—overweight, balding yet ponytailed, and with a scruffy beard and slightly askew wire-rimmed glasses—walked in. He looked groggy but cheerful rather than grouchy. "Well, it took you long enough, but you made it," he said to Judy, giving her an enthusiastic hug. "I thought you might be all talk and no action."

"You should know me better than that, Jim. If I don't mean it, I don't say it. I was just waiting for the right time. I want you to meet a very good friend of mine—Ella. She lived downstairs from me for years. This is Jim Benjamin."

Ella reached out her hand, and instead of shaking it, he gave it a dramatic, courtly kiss, bending from the waist and ending with a dramatic "ahh." Ella smiled. "Do people tell you that you look like Jerry Garcia?"

"All the time. I've never met the guy, but some of the folks I know have. They tell me I should go to a concert sometime, that it would totally freak him out. He'll think he's looking into a mirror, especially if he's stoned, which I gather he is 99.9 percent of the time."

Ella laughed. "These are my daughters, Shoshanna and Mara."

"Shalom, little ladies. How would you two like some candy? I have some sesame chews and halvah. Oh, and I just got in an order of carob-covered raisins. You've got to try them. They're in that barrel over there. Use the scoop."

"Do you have Three Musketeers?"

"Nope. Chocolate is a right-wing conspiracy."

"That's what my mom says about sugar," Shoshanna replied. "And I tell her, that sounds like my kind of conspiracy."

"Funny, little lady, but your mom is right. Who do you think is getting rich off junk food? The greedy pigs who own the candy companies. Who are most at risk of dying from clogged arteries and diabetes? Minorities. It's a class war, man. A genocide. Damn straight. It's just a sugarcoated case of corporate America versus the People."

He bent down and spoke directly to the girls, his breath a mix of standard early-morning halitosis and rusty metal. He waved his fist and nodded to Ella. "Well, you got to fight back. Power to the People! Every time you say yes to carob, you say no to Hershey's and Nestlé and piggy corporate greed."

Mara obediently took a scoop of carob-coated raisins from an open wooden barrel. "This is pretty good, Shosh," Mara said, chewing thoughtfully. "It tastes almost like chocolate only badder."

"It *is* better than chocolate, honey," Jim boomed. Shoshanna was about to tell him what Mara had actually said, but by then he had turned his attention to Judy. "Did you bring any of your hand-painted stuff down? Those hand-painted cards? You know I love that kind of artsy shit, Judy."

"Yeah. A few. They're in Ella's car. I'll go get them. Hey, I wanted to mention, Ella sells jewelry. It's really cool stuff, unique. One hundred percent recycled."

"Recycling is the next wave, baby. Save Mother Earth. Groovy. Bring it in. I'll take a look. Hey, let me try to wake Francine up. We had a couple of friends from the city stay down here last night. We dropped a couple of tabs so we're a little fuzzy. You want some coffee? I know I need some. Tea? Get your stuff, come out to the back, and meet everyone."

Shoshanna could tell Jim was what she had heard people call a "quirky character." Full of himself, a terrible listener. But after years with Adam and guys like Reed and Alex—mean-spirited opportunists looking to get high and stay high, and use the people around them to maintain their highs; the me-firsts, the me-onlys—she decided Jim was fine. His impulses were kind and generous. It was easy to see that he had a big heart to go along with his big ego.

"Stay here, girls," Ella told them, and the girls watched as she followed Judy out to the car. They returned a few minutes later, during which time the girls ate another handful of carob-coated raisins and stood mesmerized in front of a lava lamp. There was a stack of floppy suede hats, and they each grabbed one to try on in front of a round oak-framed mirror. Mara's cherub face and blond corona of hair stuck out like sun rays from the huge brim.

Shoshanna stared at her own reflection and her heart skipped a beat. Staring back at her were Adam's dark eyes, minus the menace, his full mouth, and an emerging ridge of cheekbones. Had she always looked so much like him? Was Adam what her mother saw when she looked into her daughter's face? She hoped not, but she suspected it was. Oblivious, Mara laughed and spun around. Shoshanna felt a steely stab of jealousy, that she struggled to suppress.

"Careful, Mara. You're going to knock something over."

"You're no fun, Shoshie," Mara said, taking the off the hat. Mara placed it carefully back on top of the stack.

"Were you two having fun?" Judy walked in and leaned the posters against one of the glass cases.

"I was," Mara said. "Shoshie doesn't know how to have fun."

"I just didn't want you to knock anything over, Mare."

Ella took out her bag of spoon jewelry and carefully displayed each piece on the counter. Then Jim came back in, followed by a beautiful Asian woman with perfectly symmetrical bangs and a chin-length bob, who managed to look delicate despite the fact she was wearing a man's T-shirt and oversized overalls. She appeared to be at least twenty years younger than Jim, around Ella's age.

"Hey, Francine!" Judy gave the woman a hug.

"I'm glad you finally made it down," Francine replied. "That's wild. We were just talking about you the other day, how much we dug your posters. But what I'm really digging now are the hand-painted photographs. I think they could really catch on."

"Thanks. Yeah, I'd really like to get into selling them someplace outside the Haight. It's crazy the way things have changed. Only hard-core junkies and teenybopper wannabes live there now, and they're not exactly looking to buy crafts. You were right to get out when you did. It's a bad scene.

"Oh, this is my friend Ella. She lived downstairs from me for years, and then she and her old man decided to try the commune scene in Oregon. She's back, though, and

- 68 -

these are her kids, Shoshanna and Mara. They dig your shop. Right, girls?" They nodded.

"I like the hats best," said Mara.

"That's nice," Francine said, smiling at them. "Do you want some carob-covered raisins?"

"No, thank you," said Shoshanna. "We've had some."

"If I eat any more of them, I'll frow up," said Mara. Everyone laughed.

"Kids," said Jim. "So honest. So free. Then they turn into bullshit adults."

Jim and Francine bent over to inspect Ella's jewelry. Shoshanna saw her mother take a drag from her cigarette, turning her gaze away, distant and unfocused like she was thinking about nothing in particular, but Shoshanna could see that her fingers were shaking. After several seconds of silence, Jim cleared his throat.

"Whoa," Francine said, shaking her head. "These are far out. Don't you think so, Jim?"

"Yeah," he said. "They are." Bringing a bracelet up to inspect it more closely, he held it in his hand to assess the weight. "Sterling silver, huh?" Ella nodded. "How did you get the idea?"

Ella paused and Shoshanna held her breath. Would her mother tell what she herself knew to be the truth? The truth was that Adam and a few other guys from

Sweet Earth had robbed a house in a ritzy suburb outside Portland one night when they were high on mescaline and peyote. They stole a bunch of things—a stereo, a toaster oven, money, jewelry, booze, a pantry full of canned food. Adam had grabbed the silver chest as an afterthought.

"I don't know what the hell we're going to do with this silver shit," he told Ella. "We can't pawn it or take it to the flea market because they'll trace it. Look, it's even got goddamn *initials* on it." Later that day he got the idea to melt it down, but he wasn't sure how to do it or who'd want to buy a lump of molten silver, anyway. That's when Ella came up with the idea of making jewelry. She found a jigsaw in the commune workshop and a small acetylene torch and set to work. The spoons were easily molded.

By that afternoon, she'd made bracelets for the seven women at Sweet Earth. In a matter of hours, Adam had appropriated full credit for the jewelry-making idea and was busy extracting some form of payment for each bracelet—pot, a wool sweater; one of the women traded a bracelet for sex. The irony of this was not lost on Ella. What she told Jim was: "It just kind of came to me."

Shoshanna stared at her mother. Jim was right about bullshit adults. Ella caught her daughter's eye roll and shrugged before taking another drag on her cigarette.

Shoshanna bit her lip and went back to staring at the lava lamp.

"I think we can work with both of you. Sixty percent on consignment or forty percent up front. You decide."

Ella looked at Judy. Judy grinned. "See? I told you they'd love your stuff. Here, maybe the two of us should confer. C'mon, Ella. Girls, there are some cool wind chimes over there. Check 'em out. The two of us are going to step outside to talk business."

"Like Adam," Mara whispered to Shoshanna.

Shoshanna's reaction was stunned and immediate. "What the hell are you talking about?" Then it hit her: when Adam went off to sell or buy mescaline or peyote or pot or acid or heroin, he'd say he was stepping outside to transact some business. It was drug code, and she knew it, but Mara didn't. She took a deep breath to calm herself down. "No, Mara, this isn't like Adam. Judy and Mom are selling their work to Jim and Francine."

Shoshanna strained to hear her mother's and Judy's voices through the window. Jim and Francine, in the meantime, had started right in on pricing the rings and bracelets. Shoshanna saw Judy touch her mother's arm. Ella nodded, and they came back in.

"That was quick," Jim said. "What did you decide?"

"We need the cash," Judy said. "We'll take the forty

percent up front. Truth is, the Haight's been such a bummer that we'd like to split and settle down here. There's fire damage on the first floor of my house, my lease is up at the end of the month, and the owner told me she would like nothing more than to tear the place down. Immediate cash will help out. I have a couple of debts to clear up, and Ella has a couple of mouths to feed."

"Groovy. Francine's going to do the math, okay? Figure out what we owe them, Franny. You two should keep stopping by the shop to check how the inventory's doing. And listen, Ella, I don't care if you want to sell these in Petaluma or San Mateo, even San Francisco. Just don't sell to any shops here in Half Moon Bay. I want the exclusive, okay?"

"Sure."

They walked out of the store fifteen minutes later, two hundred and seventy dollars richer. "How about some ice cream, girls?" asked Judy. "I think we can splurge, unless your mom has some political opposition to ice cream."

Shoshanna waited for Ella to say ice cream was government-sanctioned poison, something she had, in fact, said before, but instead Ella just laughed and said, "That sounds like a great idea, Jude. I'll have some too." Shoshanna felt suddenly expansive, and not just because of the thought of ice cream. It was the daring to hope that for the very first time in her whole life, maybe, just maybe things were going to be okay after all. She grabbed Mara's hand and started to skip. Mara giggled and joined in, as always, everything forgiven.

"Wait a sec, guys. I want to stop at the car to get my sweater," Ella said.

"Sweater?" Mara whined. "But Ma, it's hot."

"Well, I don't know what to tell you. I'm cold," Ella said. "It'll just take a minute." They turned the corner and were walking toward the car when Ella stopped and started edging backward behind a tree. "Shit," she hissed. "Stop walking. All of you. Back up. Shit, shit, shit."

"What's the matter..." Shoshanna began, then was silent. "Come on, Mara," she whispered. "Don't look. Just turn around and let's walk back to the shop. Come on, Ma. Don't freak out. Just turn around casually, keep walking..."

When they got around the corner, Judy led them into a narrow alley between the dry cleaners and a bookstore. Ella was shaking all over. "Okay, Ella, so you saw some cops. They were writing you a ticket," Judy said. "It's a bummer and I guess I was totally wrong about them not caring, but I don't get why you're so freaked out."

"I told you that wasn't a space!" Ella hissed. "I told you. Shit. Damn it. I'm screwed."

"Yeah, sorry," Judy replied. "Seriously, though, cool it. I'll pay the fine."

"That isn't it," Ella said. "Sweet Earth reported the car stolen. I know they did. They're after us. Whether I get thrown in jail for car theft, or they find us and haul our asses back to Oregon, we're screwed."

"Why would you think those freak burnouts are that organized? They probably figured you were gone, said some horrible things about you, made some idle threats, went into a field to smoke enough dope to get their blood pressure down, dropped some acid, had an orgy, then forgot all about it."

"They only have one car, Jude. They have an old truck that doesn't even work. They need the car. They would probably kill me if they could get to me. You don't know them. You don't know what they're like. They're *psychos*, man."

Shoshanna touched her mother's quivering arm. "Listen, you got to calm down, Ma. Judy's right. They aren't that organized. Plus, the last people Sweet Earthers are gonna want to talk to are the police. Adam is always saying he hates the pigs. They all do. They don't want the law looking into what they're doing." Even though she was talking with conviction, in her gut, Shoshanna wondered if there would ever be a place far enough away that they could stop being afraid.

"Are we still getting ice cream?" Mara asked.

"Not now, Mara!" Ella's voice was harsh.

Shoshanna saw the tears pooling in her sister's eyes. "In a little while, Mara. Right now we have to take care of this problem. But soon." Shoshanna rested a hand on her sister's shoulder and Mara nodded her head sullenly.

Ella was oblivious to Mara's response. She was still in full panic mode. Shoshanna thought she could actually see her mother's heart pounding through the thin skin of her bony chest. Shoshanna turned toward Judy. "Okay. Judy, could you walk out there and check if the cops are still at the car? If they just wrote a ticket, we'll drive back to your place. If they're still there, walk by and try to see what they're doing. We'll stay here."

Shoshanna reached over and put her arm around Ella. "Ma, it's probably nothing. Probably just a ticket, and now that we've got money, we'll pay it. It's going to be okay."

"Then we'll get some ice cream?" Mara asked. Ella sighed.

Ten minutes later, Judy returned, looking uncharacteristically grim. "You're right, El. The car was reported stolen."

"Shit," Ella moaned. "I knew it. We're dead."

"Wait. It gets weirder. I started talking to one of the cops, and he told me that not only was it reported stolen, but they've been looking for it for months. He radioed in the license plate number and they told him to impound the vehicle. Someone saw it leaving the scene of a robbery in Corvallis, and it was also involved in a fatal hit-and-run outside Grants Pass where some old dude got killed and his body was dumped down a ravine. When I was standing there, they were saying it looked like there was dried blood in the trunk."

"Adam told me that was engine oil…" Ella's voice trailed off.

"Right. Honest Adam," Shoshanna whispered to herself.

Judy continued, "And to top it all off, as they were getting ready to tow it, two handguns and a bag of heroin popped out from under the left-rear wheel well. I knew Adam was crazy and messed up, but I had no idea he was that kind of crazy and messed up."

Shoshanna looked at Judy. "We did. At least, me and my mom did. That's why we had to get out of there. We tried to make it a game for Mara and all, but we knew."

"We knew, and trust me, it's the tip of the iceberg." Ella slid down the trunk of the tree she'd been leaning against and onto the asphalt curb, her head between her knees. Mara sat down next to her, dejectedly contemplating how close they'd gotten to having ice cream.

"I hate to say it, El, but you're not going to get that car back. We should go to Jim and Francine's and figure out what to do. They're cool. They'll put you up for a while. I can bum a ride with them or hitch back home and pack up, then come back here."

"Half Moon Bay," Ella said. "A half hour ago it seemed like the perfect place to live. Now I'm just hoping it's a safe place to disappear."

Shoshanna was hoping the same thing. In her head, she found herself repeating the phrase her mother had told them for years, a phrase that now carried an ominous ring of truth: Adam has radar.

CHAPTER FOUR

For the next few days, they lay low. Francine drove Judy back to San Francisco to close up her apartment, and Jim set to putting them up in the basement of the store. Ella liked the fact that, being a cellar, there were no windows and thick cinder-block walls. They made her feel safe. "Like being in a bomb shelter," she told Shoshanna and Mara. "We're going underground." She spent the first day reading magazines and chain-smoking on the threadbare sofa that also served as her bed.

Shoshanna tried to make it an adventure for Mara, gamely telling stories and even playing endless games of Go Fish and slapjack. After a few hours it started to grow tiresome for both of them. Shoshanna longed to go outside and breathe fresh air. Jim said he'd bring her out in the yard after dark "to get some oxygen," and he did. Shoshanna stood on a patch of bare earth for five minutes, taking in lungfuls of air that carried a salty trace of ocean, and looked at the stars before sighing and following Jim back down.

Francine brought them paper and pencils, which occupied them for a while. Shoshanna started to go through the magazine stash. She had no idea so much was going on in the world. She knew that everyone at Sweet Earth hated Nixon and railed against cops, the military-industrial complex, and conformity, but now she saw all of these terms for what they were from a different, less insular perspective.

After she finished *Time* and *Newsweek,* she started looking at the fashion magazines. She'd never used or even thought about curlers and mouthwash and deodorant, tampons and lip gloss. These were foreign items to someone like herself, raised so far outside the mainstream. It was strange to think of women having to shave their legs or wearing bras. When she went up the stairs to use the bathroom, she looked in the mirror, imagining how she'd look in bangs. What would it be like to go to a department store and buy a new dress? Something with flowers, a high waist, and what they were calling "Juliet sleeves."

Three times a day, Jim or Francine brought down food, which was a strange mix of healthy, organic fare and convenience-store junk. Tofu and bean casserole would be washed down with orange soda and served with a side of potato chips. Jim even went out and bought them a carton of vanilla ice cream. After Mara told him she'd never eaten ice cream, he said that the thought of a childhood without ice cream blew his mind. Shoshanna loved eating the ice cream, but not as much as she loved watching her sister's blissful expression as she ate herself into a stomachache. That night, the girls fell asleep on a pile of old blankets, while Ella just fell asleep where she'd been sitting all day on the couch.

"Here, girls. Entertainment for the troops," Jim said on the morning of day two, coming slowly down the creaky wooden stairs with an armful of merchandise. He coughed. "Jesus, how do you breathe in here? There's no ventilation."

The girls looked up. "We're used to it." Shoshanna shrugged. "Everyone smoked at Sweet Earth except the kids." She was going to add that cigarette smoke smelled a whole lot better than pot or, even worse, hashish, but decided to keep that to herself.

"Thank you for bringing us presents again!" shouted Mara. "I love you."

"And I love you too, little ray of sunshine," Jim replied, watching her walk away with a box of animal crackers.

"Here," he said, handing Ella a newspaper and a pack of Marlboros. "For you. Though I really think you should be spending more time eating and less time smoking. You didn't touch the tofu casserole the other night, Ella, and that's not healthy. Look at you—you're skin and bones. I know, I know, you have free will, and who am I to give you a lecture, but I'm a worrier. Suit yourself, but please, for the sake of your girls, eat. Oh, and check out the local newspaper. I thought you might find the front page interesting."

Abandoned Car Traced to Oregon Commune

An apparently abandoned car ticketed for a parking violation on Main Street in Half Moon Bay has been traced to Sweet Earth Farm, a hippie commune in Cave Junction, Oregon. Sweet Earth Farm has gained notoriety for its philosophy of political anarchy, free love, and rampant drug use. The car contained two bags of heroin with a street value of more than twenty thousand dollars, two forty-five-caliber handguns, and a hunting knife.

Human blood, which has been traced to a hit-and-run incident, was also found on the front bumper and in the trunk of the car.

The commune had reported the car missing four days ago. During the routine background check after the parking violation, Half Moon Bay police notified authorities in Portland. Portland police linked the car to several area burglaries, as well as the hit-and-run death of Edwin Neville, 76, a retired farmer from Grants Pass, Oregon. Neville had been struck several weeks ago on a rural road. His body was found days later at the bottom of a ravine. Traces of Neville's blood were found on the right headlight and bumper of the car, as well as in the car's trunk.

Police arrested commune members Reed Stovall, Alexander McNeil, Barbara (aka Melaya) Levine, Chandra Johnson, Mark Treborne, and Stevenson

Vanderbilt on drug possession and weapons charges. They will be arraigned in Portland Superior Court on Friday.

Police have yet to determine how the car arrived in Half Moon Bay. There is speculation that Adam Ebersole, founder and leader of the Sweet Earth Farm commune and a convicted drug dealer, drove the car as far as Half Moon Bay and continued on foot. Mr. Ebersole is described as six-foot-two, with a slender build and dark brown, shoulder-length hair. He has a three-inch scar on his forehead and may or may not have a beard. Anyone who has seen any person matching this description is asked to call the Half Moon Bay Police Department. Mr. Ebersole may be armed and should be considered extremely dangerous.

Ella read intently, her brow furrowed. "I don't get it. How could he have just vanished?"

Jim shook his head. "No one knows. Do you really think he'd follow you down here?"

"I wouldn't be surprised at anything Adam did," Ella said.

"Adam has radar," said Mara, licking her animal cracker crumb-covered fingertips. "Right?"

"That's what we say," Ella told Jim, lighting up another cigarette. "Who knows? He could be in Canada, or he could be hiding upstairs." She exhaled, shaking her head. "Even if he's not here, he's here." She first pointed to her head and then opened her arms to signify everywhere. "Like God."

"More like Satan," Shoshanna said. "Can I read the paper?"

"Knock yourself out," Ella said, handing it over. "I hate to say it's not gonna shock you. There's so much shit that's happened that didn't get reported."

"Man, I feel sorry for you guys," Jim said.

"Yeah. It's been tough, and I don't know why I thought we could just up and leave. Hey, I never thanked you for all you and Francine are doing. You have been so incredible to us, feeding us and giving the girls all these things and letting us crash here. You really put yourselves out for us."

"Just humans being human, Ella. Taking care of each other. Peace and love. Listen, I wanted to tell you a couple of things. One, I sold all but two of the bracelets and one of the rings you gave me. People are crazy about them. When you get yourself set up, I'd like to buy some more."

Ella smiled. "Wow. That's groovy. Sure. Cool."

"Oh, and Judy called. She's on her way down here with all her stuff in a U-Haul. I'm going with her to find a place for you all when she gets in."

"No shit! That's great, man. Thanks. Hey, girls, are you gonna thank Jim for all he's done?" Ella lit a fresh cigarette with the butt of the cigarette she'd just finished.

"Thanks, Jim. And thanks to Francine too, even though she's not here," Shoshanna said. "I made you both a card. I'm not much of an artist but it has your pictures on it."

"I love it. I look young and super hip. Kind of like Charlie Brown with a ponytail and a dashiki. I really dig the hair, nice comb-over. You'd never guess I'm going bald. Aren't you going to sign it, Shoshie?"

"Why?"

"All great artists sign their work."

"I don't think it's great art, but I'm happy to sign it."

"You've got neat handwriting. Must've been paying attention when they taught you handwriting in school."

"I've never been to school. I learned this myself. Well, some of the women at Sweet Earth helped me. And this girl named Moonbeam. She went to school for a few years and she was really good at cursive."

"Wait. You never went to school?"

Shoshanna shook her head.

Jim looked at Ella, incredulous. "Vaccines," she said. "You can't go to school without them, but screw that. There's been lots of research that says they're not good for you. It's one of Big Brother's most invasive conspiracies. The government's pandering to the drug companies."

He shook his head. "I don't know about that, Ella, but I do know a kid Shoshie's age—how old are you?"

"Fourteen."

"You should be in high school, babe. How the hell are you going to learn about the world? Make friends?"

Ella took a drag, exhaled, and leaned her head back against the couch, her eyes closed. "You don't know, man... the place we're from...where we were before that...it was, like...Forget it, man, never mind." She closed her eyes, leaned her head back, and sighed. "You wouldn't understand. It wasn't like anything the outside world could teach had any relevance."

"That's messed up, Ella. Shoshie, when you settle here, you gotta go to school."

"So she can be brainwashed by the Establishment?"

Shoshanna looked at Jim and shrugged.

"I'm not here to argue. You're right, I don't know your trip. I only know mine." Shaking his head, he turned to give Mara a hug. "And you, little buttercup. I'm happy to see pencils and paper put to such good use. What a beautiful flower."

"It's for you." Mara handed it to him and gave him a kiss on the cheek.

After Jim went back upstairs, Shoshanna walked over to the couch and sat next to her mother. "Jim's right. I should be in school. If it wasn't for Indigo and that kid Bilbo's mom and the teacher at the Free School in San Francisco, I wouldn't know how to read and write. I wouldn't be good at math. I had to pick up everything on my own."

"I'm tired, Shosh." Ella's voice went flat. "Have you seen my matches?"

"You dropped them under the couch. They're right next to your foot." Shoshanna knew there was no point in talking to Ella when she got like this. It was a battle for another day.

Shoshanna and Mara passed the rest of the day in what felt like a smoky cocoon. Going up the narrow stairs to use the bathroom provided them with the only clue as to what time it was. If they could hear the voices of customers, they knew it was before five, which was when the shop closed. A bit later on they went upstairs and heard no voices, so they knew it had to be close to dinnertime.

They wandered back and played a few hands of Go Fish. Mara drew some more. Shoshie read about how to transition her winter wardrobe into spring. (Switch that turtleneck for a pastel T-shirt under that jumper!) They waited. Their stomachs rumbled.

"Jim and Francine are late, Ma. I'm getting hungry," Mara said.

Shoshanna was too, though she didn't say anything, not wanting to set her mom off. Instead, she lay back on the heap of blankets and let out a gusty sigh. "We'll get something to eat soon enough, Mara. Just be patient."

"I can't do anything about it anyway," Ella murmured.

Just then, the door opened, which made the three of them jump. Footsteps could be heard coming down the stairs. "Judy!" Mara jumped into Judy's arms, almost knocking her off her feet.

"Hey, Mara. Man, is it good to see you! It's good to see you all. Whoa, you guys have really made a nest for yourselves down here. Too bad there's no oxygen. God damn, Ella, I can hardly see through this smoke."

"Sorry. How did the move go?"

"I'm beat, but it's over. Guess what? I found us a place to stay."

"That fast?"

"Well, Jim took me out to see a friend of his, this guy Avery Elliot. He's—I don't know—old, like in his seventies, kind of eccentric, but he's got a decent-sized vegetable farm and he grows artichokes, beans, and turnips and probably some other stuff. I saw some pesticides in his storage shed so I doubt he's into the organic scene but we could steer him in that direction, huh, Francine?" Francine nodded, smiling.

"He does some business with local grocery stores, Safeway and Lucky, and he's trying to start up a roadside stand in a shed he owns that's right next to the road. I guess he has some disease and he could use some help on the farm. His son lives in L.A., and even though Avery has begged him, the son refuses to come home to lend a hand. So Avery was feeling pretty desperate, like he was going to have to sell the farm.

"He mentioned the situation to Jim at the local diner a few days ago, and that's where we come in. We're going to help Avery with his crop, work in the fields for the harvest, and get the roadside stand up and running in exchange for a place to live."

"Cool," Ella said, reaching for a cigarette. Her voice held not the slightest trace of enthusiasm. Shoshanna was used to this; Ella dealt with stress and panic by underreacting. She knew other people must think Ella was unemotional and weird, but those other people hadn't seen Ella get punched around the room so hard her jaw was dislocated and ribs broken for raising her voice or just questioning Adam.

"It *is* cool, but to be honest, it's not going to be all that comfortable at the beginning. I mean, I saw the place where we'll be living. It has electricity and running water. There's a bathroom and appliances in the kitchen. It's still basically a barn, though."

"A barn?" Shoshanna was not thrilled about escaping from one farm just to move to another.

"Yeah. But don't worry. It's not like we'll be sleeping in a silo or a horse stall. This is a barn with real rooms in it. I think it was used to store machinery, and it smells kind of like gasoline and fertilizer. But don't worry. We can make it nice. We just have to clean it up."

Ella rubbed her eyes. "Clean it up? Man, I'm so tired."

"Well, it's not like we're going over there now, Ma. It's already dark," Shoshanna said.

"Right. We'll leave tomorrow morning. Francine and Jim said they'd drive us," Judy added. "For now, El, just rest."

A barn. Shoshanna thought of the barns back at Sweet Earth Farm. There were five, but three of them had rotted out to the point of partial collapse. The two that you could actually walk in weren't fit for a human being to live in by any stretch of the imagination. One was home to the two cows, one horse, and nine goats Sweet Earth owned, and no one ever wanted to muck it out, so the barn was ankle-deep in animal crap, pee, and flies. You could smell the barn, which was a hundred yards away, from inside the house.

The other barn was used for apple storage and sorting. It was less than ten years old and cheaply constructed of aluminum sheeting. Even though it wasn't remotely clean or organized, it was big and dry and had long rows of fluorescent lights and a working conveyor belt. That was where Ella, Shoshanna, and Mara spent their post-harvest days, sorting and crating apples.

The barn wasn't homey, but it was safe, and because the other Sweet Earthers had other things they wanted to do with their time, the barn gave the three some measure of privacy, as well as a form of worth to the commune. They knew the importance of what they did. As long as they were productive, they weren't disposable. It was a terrible but true equation.

Mara had no interest in moving to the barn. "Why can't we just stay here?" she asked. "This is fine."

"Jim and Francine have been really cool about having the three of us stay here, but they can't keep us here forever. Besides, you should be outside playing in fresh air." Shoshanna gave her sister a forced half smile.

Shoshanna knew she and her mother and sister couldn't just hide out in Jim and Francine's basement forever. But she also knew, after reading the newspaper, that Adam was out there somewhere, and that the cops were looking for them too. She'd seen what cops did to hippies when they'd busted Sweet Earth on several occasions. They had to keep moving between the law and the lawless. A rock and a hard place. A barn that didn't even look like a house sounded like as good a place as any.

A half hour later, Judy, Jim, and Francine brought them upstairs into the store. They put a blanket down on the wood-planked floor, lit candles, and ordered takeout pizza. It was supposed to be a going-away party—at least that's what Francine and Jim called it—but Ella was in no mood to celebrate. She just sat there smoking, looking pale and twitchy, and glancing furtively at the doors and windows. The sound of someone on the sidewalk outside caused her to gasp. She didn't relax until they were in the basement again with the door closed.

Judy came down the stairs the next morning, smelling like minty toothpaste and Ivory soap. Shoshanna was already awake, reading about how to control acne. She smiled at Judy and inhaled deeply, thinking, *That's what I'm going to smell like when we settle into our home. Toothpaste.*

Clean. Not cigarettes and weed and sweat. Judy bent down and kissed Shoshanna's and Mara's cheeks.

"Good morning, sweeties. Time to get up and get dressed." She touched Ella's shoulder. "C'mon, Ella. Rise and shine." Ella groaned. "Fine, then. At least rise. We've got to go. Francine's waiting."

Still groggy, they trudged upstairs. Mara tripped on the lip of the top step and fell, skinning her knee. Ordinarily she would have made the dramatic most of the moment, wailing and requesting a newly discovered commodity—a Band-Aid—but now she just got up and kept moving despite the trickle of blood, not yet alert enough to cry.

Francine stood at the front door. "Hi, ladies! It's going to be a beautiful day. The universe is smiling on you. The sun is just beginning to come up. Let's go check out your new pad."

The cool morning air washed over them as they followed Francine to the car. The sun broke through the gray, early-morning fog. Seabirds squawked, and somewhere in the distance they could hear a lonesome train whistle. They piled in, Judy in front with Francine, and Mara and Shoshanna on either side of Ella in the backseat so they could look out the windows.

"Sorry Jim's not around to see you off," Francine said, starting the engine. "He was up late writing in his journal.

Sometimes he gets so excited about an idea that he can't sleep, so he starts writing it down. I bet he didn't crash until a couple of hours ago. He'll come out to visit you when you're all settled in."

The early-morning sky lightened to a faded blue. They started off down Main Street, the windows open to let in the morning air, which seemed to shift whimsically between cool and downright chilly. At times, Shoshanna could see her breath if she pushed the air out from down deep enough in her lungs. Judy and Francine were talking in the front seat, their voices low.

Suddenly, the wail of a siren split the calm morning air. Turning around, Shoshanna saw the red flashing light of the police cruiser and noticed her mother's reaction, which was to clutch at her chest and sink lower into her seat.

"Damn cops. What do they want? I was going, like, twenty miles an hour. We've got to pull over," Francine said.

"That's it," Ella said. "They must have found Adam. They must want to take me in too. It's all over."

"Relax, Ella," Judy said. "They probably saw us get in and figured they'd hassle the hippies."

Shoshanna and Mara held on to their mother's hands and tried to soothe her. "You'll be okay, Ma," Mara said.

Ella just sat and stared at the floor, her nervous fingers, nails bitten to the quick, tugging at the fringe of her llama bag while she talked to herself in an unintelligible whisper.

A policeman, blond and young, came up to Francine and asked for her license and registration, which she handed over. "You're getting an early start," he said. "Where are you peace-and-love folks going?"

"To visit an old friend at the shore," Francine said. "He has a farm and we thought the girls here would like to see the animals."

"You hippies. You can never get enough nature, can you?"

Francine didn't lose her temper. Instead, she smiled at the policeman. "No, officer, we can't."

"The reason I am stopping you is that your left taillight is out. I mean, that's the reason I'm authorized to stop you. My partner called in your plates to make sure this car is really yours, ma'am."

"The car belongs to my husband."

"So it does," said the other cop. "James Benjamin." He looked at Francine. "Looks like Jim got himself an Ono."

"Racist pig," Judy whispered under her breath. The cop looked over, his expression indicating he didn't hear. "You're a pretty one," he said, then returned to the police car and was talking to his partner for several minutes. Ella kept repeating that they were screwed, and Shoshanna kept trying—in vain—to calm her mother down.

"Ma, even if Adam did all that shit the cops were talking about, you weren't there when it happened. You didn't know."

"Watch your mouth, Shosh. And, no, I wasn't there for it but I knew. At least I knew about some of it."

Francine turned around and looked at Ella. "Listen, if you relax, they won't even talk to you. I'm just going to say you guys are friends of mine from San Francisco. They have nothing on any of us. Our biggest problem now is you acting paranoid, like you killed somebody. Stay cool, Ella."

"She's right, Ma. Just relax," Shoshanna said, even though her own heart was pounding and her stomach churning. "We'll be okay." She looked in the rearview mirror and could see both cops sauntering up to the car, the young blond cop joined by a short, balding officer with a belly that hung over his belt.

"Okay, Miss Lee," the bald cop said. "This checks out. But I got to tell you, here's the real reason we stopped you. You have a little problem." Shoshanna felt her mother's grip tighten again and watched her thin face turn even paler. "I know you and Mr. Benjamin own that psychedelic store in town. Turns out Officer Tolbert's wife, Cheryl, got a bracelet from the shop a couple of days ago. A friend of hers bought it. It was made from a sterling silver spoon.

Monogrammed. Officer Tolbert, being the vigilant officer he is, ran a stolen goods check on it, and turns out it was stolen. There was a home invasion in Portland, and we're pretty sure Adam Ebersole and the Sweet Earth family pulled it off.

"Officer Franklin and I can't help but put two and two together, Miss Lee. You sell a stolen spoon from Ebersole's heist—a heist in which the homeowner was tied up and beaten—in your little shop, and Ebersole's car is found on the street around the corner from you. Kind of a weird coincidence. It makes us suspect that you might know something about Ebersole's whereabouts."

Francine looked at both of the cops and shook her head. "Listen. Jim and I run a clean business. I bought those bracelets from some craftsperson who wanted the money up front, and that's what I gave her. She didn't tell me her name or where she was from. She mentioned she got her materials from pawn shops. I think that's where you should be looking. I don't know Ebersole at all, although he sounds like a really sketchy dude. I hope you catch him. But today, if you don't mind, I'd like to get my friends and these two lovely girls to the beach."

The cops looked at Francine, then over at Judy. They peered into the backseat to look at Ella and the girls.

Shoshanna, used to acting innocent from "family fun and games," did her best to appear relaxed. Mara smiled at the men. "We're going to see the ocean," she said. "And a barn."

Officer Franklin smiled back. "Aren't you a cutie. Here's a warning about the taillight, Miss Lee. Get it fixed. And just so's you know, we got our eye on you. Ebersole's a dangerous character, like Charlie Manson. A real sick bastard. Sorry, kids. We don't want him wreaking havoc in Half Moon Bay."

This was her father they were talking about. A sick bastard. A twisted psychopath like Charles Manson, who had encouraged his followers to go on a drug-fueled murder spree. To think Adam had held her in his arms, could even be kind to her. To think his blood ran through her veins. Shoshanna shuddered.

"Are we good to go, officer?" Francine asked.

"Yeah. I guess so. But like I said, we're keeping an eye on you."

They drove off past the library, the schools, and the police station before turning onto the highway.

"Are you okay, Shoshie?" Mara asked, looking into her sister's face.

"I'm fine," Shoshanna said. "Or I will be, if you quit picking your nose." She stuck out her tongue and Mara giggled.

"I hate the pigs," Ella said. "They're always hassling us. And now they're gonna hassle you, Francine. I'm really sorry for bring this shit on you."

Francine shrugged. "Jim and I are going to be okay. We're very careful, and the cops have bigger fish to fry, like Adam. And don't you worry. You're going to be totally safe. Avery's farm is in the middle of nowhere."

"Maybe Adam's radar won't work there," Shoshanna said, trying in vain to coax a smile from Ella.

They had been driving for only ten minutes or so when Mara started to whine. "Are we almost there?"

"We'll be there soon," Francine said. "Look out at the ocean, Mara. You might see a whale."

"Really?" Shoshanna asked.

"Well, it's possible, but to tell you the truth, probably not, unless your eyes are really good. There have been whale sightings a little farther offshore. This part of the coast is on their migration path."

Shoshanna noticed the coast of California was different from the coast of Oregon. Oregon was rockier with lots of pine trees, and the shores were peppered with coves or inlets, so it felt more sheltered, almost like being at a lake. Here, the gently rolling grasslands sloped and ended at a narrow stretch of sandy beach, which led to the vast slate-gray waters of the Pacific.

"Why is there more sky here than in Oregon?" Mara asked.

"There isn't more sky. It just looks that way because there are fewer trees and the ground is flatter," Shoshanna explained.

"It's pretty, isn't it?" Judy asked.

"Uh-huh," Mara said. "Can we see the ocean from the barn where we're supposed to live?"

"No," Francine told her. "It's not right on the water, but it's close. You can walk to the ocean in ten minutes. Maybe less."

They drove along the coast for a bit longer before turning inland off the main road. Shoshanna could see farmhouses and fields, and they passed a couple of stores (Hank's Used Cars, Half Moon Sundries) before they came to a dirt road. There was a handmade wooden sign with uneven letters painted in faded green: Elliot's Farm, 1/4 mile. Right on the corner, next to the road, a large, ramshackle shed listed precariously to the right. Along its front was a tattered green-and-white-striped awning. "That's the roadside stand Avery's trying to get started," Francine said. "It could really use some help. I have a feeling you'll all be spending some time there this summer if he gets his way."

The car bumped and rattled down the rutted dirt road, raising clouds of dust. "Are we almost there?" Mara asked repeatedly.

"Enough, Mara!" Ella exhaled.

Shoshanna reached behind Ella to tickle her sister's arm. Mara started to squeal, but the sight of a small, white-frame farmhouse distracted her into silence.

"There it is," Judy announced. "That's Avery's place. The barn is just behind it."

The house was unadorned, plain and boxy, a single story with a dormered roof topped by black shingles. Shoshanna thought it looked dejected, despite the neatly mowed yard with its decorative tiny windmill, painted a jaunty red. There were no curtains on any of the windows, no flowers in the garden, only green shrubs cut low and square across the top.

"The barn we'll be living in is around the back," Judy said.

The barn was not what any of them expected. Unlike the barns at Sweet Earth, it was sturdy and massive, easily five times the size of the house. It looked old, but structurally well maintained. Some years ago, maybe a decade judging from the amount of fading and peeling, someone had painted the barn a deep red.

"This is where we're going to live?" asked Mara. "It doesn't look like a people house."

"I know it doesn't, but there are rooms on the ground

floor. Up above are just a hayloft and storage," Judy told her. "We'll go in and I'll show you, Mara. Thanks, Francine, for bringing us out. We can take it from here. I know you have to get back to open the store."

"I do have to get back, but I have a little time. Let me help you unload."

They didn't have much to bring in. There were pillows and blankets that Jim and Francine had given them, some of them brand-new, plus a bag of assorted clothes that Judy had picked up at a Salvation Army store just to tide them over. Francine took a paper bag out of the trunk and handed it to Shoshanna.

"These are for both of you girls from me and Jim. Mostly they're the things you've already used—see, Mara? There's the doll you liked. Shoshie, there are two decks of cards and all those *Seventeen* and *Glamour* magazines. There's some candy in there too. And here's the important thing. At the bottom, under the doll, there are books. Picture books for you, Mara. Shoshie, these other books are for you. Jim wanted you to have them. There are pencils and pens and lots of paper too.

"I talked to Judy and she promised me that she and your mom would work on teaching Mara to read. So you can do some reading and writing over the next couple of months before school starts in the fall. There's a math book in there, basic algebra. Oh, and a science book. Jim and I are hoping your mom will change her mind about school. Half Moon Bay has a pretty good public high school, and he thinks you should go."

"Thank you." Shoshanna gave Francine a hug. "I hope I can convince my mom. She's not big on changing her mind when it comes to stuff with too many rules."

"We can always hope," Francine said. "You have the summer to work on her."

"Thanks, Francine," Judy said, walking over and giving her a hug. "I don't honestly know what we would have done without you and Jim. I hope we didn't get you into any trouble with the cops."

"We'll be fine," Francine told her. "Don't worry."

Then the four of them stood by the side of the barn, their new home, and watched Francine drive off slowly down the driveway, Shoshanna and Mara waving wildly.

"Well," Judy said, pulling a key out of her pocket. "Want to see our house?"

"Yes!" shrieked Mara, running ahead.

Unlocking the door, Judy led them down a narrow hallway and into a small room. It looked like it had once been an office. Warped, fake dark-brown walnut paneling stretched from floor to ceiling, and the floor was covered in a stained gold carpet. Orange burlap-covered partitions chopped the space into four tiny cubicles, each with a desk and two black vinyl chairs. Fluorescent lights suspended from the rafters cast a sick-green glow and made a humming sound that made Shoshanna grit her teeth. The air was stale and smelled of years of unchecked decay and mildew.

"You'll have to use your imagination," Judy told Ella. "They turned this into office space a few years back when Avery's son, Dave, worked here and had this idea to start a mail-order seed business. It never panned out, I guess. See, if we knock the cubicles down—which is no big deal because they're not really attached to anything—this can be the living room. We'll have to get rid of this gross carpeting, though. I'm hoping the wood underneath is in decent shape. I think it'll be nice when we take the cubicles out." Ella looked unconvinced.

"Don't worry. The rest of the place won't require so much imagination, just elbow grease. It used to be an apartment. Avery's son Dave lived here when he was setting up and running the seed business."

Judy opened another door and they walked into the small kitchen. The counters and floor were thick with grease and grime, but underneath the dirt they could see all of the necessary appliances were there: a stove, an old refrigerator, and a pitted porcelain sink with running water. The wallpaper—a pattern of Amish men in brimmed hats and women in bonnets in buggies, interspersed with Pennsylvania Dutch hex signs—was peeling off the walls in strips, and the white metal drawers and cabinets had begun to rust. The green-and-white-checkerboard linoleum floor was pitted and gritty.

"Yeah, I know. It's ugly as hell but everything works," Judy offered.

Shoshanna saw the potential. "And we can put a little table in here—well, it would have to be a really little table—but we could do that and eat here. There's a nice view of the fields from the window over the sink, don't you think? And that tree out there by the kitchen door is perfect for a swing for Mara."

Judy smiled. "Okay, next, we have bedroom number one." She opened the door into the biggest room yet. Amazingly, a double bed and a night table were already in place, plain, heavy oak pieces in good condition. Shoshanna felt a smile creep over her face while Mara screamed in delight.

"A television!" yelled Mara running over to the tiny black box sitting on a plastic cart with wheels in the corner of the room.

"Don't get too excited, Mara. I'm not even sure that thing works. It looks pretty old," Judy said. Shoshanna walked over and plugged it in. Flicking on the switch, she was greeted by the sound of static. "You've got to adjust the antenna..." Judy told her, moving the rabbit-ear wires into position. A game show wavered into view, fuzzy but discernible.

"Our own television!" Mara shouted. "I get to choose the shows!"

"Said who?" Shoshanna tried to find another channel, to no avail. "Looks like our choice is limited. Or non-existent."

"That's for the best," Ella said. "They don't call it a boob tube for nothing."

Judy clapped her hands. "Okay, here's something that you'll really get some use out of: the bathroom. There's no tub but there's a shower. Gross, look at that green stuff growing in there! *Ugh.* It looks like moss. God, I think it is moss. Oh, well, nothing a little bleach can't take care of. Oh, Shoshie and Mara, this is important—the toilet doesn't work. It doesn't flush for some reason. For the time being, you have to just go outside in the yard until I figure out what's wrong. Avery knows it's broken, and he said he'd go to the hardware store to get the parts it needs.

"Okay, then. Moving on, right over here is bedroom number two. Just like bedroom number one but smaller and with no closet or bathroom. I figure I can sleep there. And right next to it is bedroom three. That's yours, Ella. I thought you'd like this room because it's quiet and you can lock the door. You and I can share the bathroom in the hall. There's a shower and a toilet that needs to be replaced, but Avery promised he'd get it done by tomorrow."

Ella looked like a sleepwalker, roused against her will from a deep sleep. She glanced around, managed a wan smile, and sighed. "It's nice, Judy. Really nice. I'm really grateful for you finding us a place to stay and all, but damn, there's so much for us to do. It's kind of overwhelming."

"We can do it, Ma," Shoshanna said. "Think about it. It's got enough bedrooms and some furniture and even a TV. The kitchen just needs to be cleaned up. Plus, it's all ours. We won't have new people showing up all the time, crashing on the couch and burning holes in the furniture. It's a million times better than anything we had at Sweet Earth."

"I know it's better here, Shosh. I'm not an idiot." Ella opened her bag and began rummaging around for another cigarette. "It's just that at Sweet Earth fixing things wasn't my problem. I had other problems."

"No one fixed anything there, Ma. Remember?" Shoshanna said. "Everything just stayed broken. No one worked except us. We are really good at working, in case you forgot. And the other thing you seem to be forgetting is that there's no Adam here. It's just us, living in a barn in back of someone's house in the middle of nowhere. We're safe."

Mara joined in. "We're safe and we don't have to share the bathroom with everyone, plus it's inside instead of in the yard. Me and Shoshie can clean. We're good at cleaning. I bet Judy's good at cleaning too."

"I am." Judy nodded. "Plus, seems to me," she said as she opened the window, "that if you could get through all the horrible shit you had to get through at Sweet Earth, cleaning up this place will be a snap."

Ella opened the back door and looked outside. "That *is* a nice tree." She leaned against the counter, swaying slightly, and shut her eyes. "I don't know what's wrong with me. It's weird. It's like I had all this adrenaline in me when I was trying to get out of Oregon, and now that we're here, I've lost steam. I just feel so tired all of a sudden. It's like there are too many things to think about. Too many things to do. And I wish the cops didn't have the car. What if they find my fingerprints in it and come after me?"

"Don't worry about that, Ella. It's not like you're a fugitive from justice. You just had the crap luck to fall in love and marry one," Judy said. "You've got to trust me on this."

"Judy's right, Ma. This is good. We're in a really good place. You're just worn out. So take it slow until you feel stronger." Shoshanna moved close enough to put her hand on her mother's shoulder. "But give this place a chance, Ma. For yourself. For us."

Ella sighed and shrugged Shoshanna's hand off her shoulder, like it was a weight she couldn't bear instead of a comfort. "I know you're right. It's just I have kind of a headache. Maybe I need to lie down."

"Go ahead," Judy said. "Stretch out on the bed in your room. We'll get started on fixing things up. Shosh, Mare, let's go. We're going to clean this place from top to bottom. You won't even recognize it after we're through."

Ella didn't argue. She went into her room. Shoshanna heard her slide the lock into place.

They walked with Judy across the backyard to Avery's house to get cleaning supplies. He'd left the back door open, along with a scrawled note written on a napkin on the kitchen table and tucked under the salt shaker. "Wow. I can barely read his handwriting," Judy said. "It's really shaky."

"Want me to try?" Shoshanna asked. Judy handed it to her.

Dear Judy:

Please help yourself to cleaning supplies under the sink. The mop and bucket and broom are by the back door. Tomorrow you can start fixing up the roadside stand. I have gone to get paint and the parts for the toilet and order the new toilet. Since you don't have a car, I will go to town for groceries. I should be home around noon. Welcome to Elliot's Farm.

Avery

"That's so nice," Shoshanna said.

"He's a nice man. You'll like him. He just seems kind of sad. He has something called Parkinson's disease, which is a sickness that makes him shake and he can't control the shaking. It's really tough on him. I'm hoping he'll cheer up with you two cuties around. I know he'll be relying on us to get the harvest in and sold."

Together, they found the broom and mop, a nearly full gallon jug of bleach, some ammonia, and something called Comet that Judy said would work for the bathroom, along with some sponges and a roll of paper towels. "This ought to do it," Judy said. "Man. Look at this. Avery's kitchen is so neat. We'll never get ours this clean, I'm telling you now."

Shoshanna had to agree. "It's neat, but it doesn't really seem like a kitchen. Sweet Earth's kitchen was really gross and messy and people always left dirty things lying around, but you could tell people used it for cooking. This kitchen doesn't have any food or dishes or pots and pans. It doesn't smell like anyone cooks here, ever. It just smells like soap."

"I bet there are no rats or possums, though," Mara said.

"You had rats and possums in your kitchen?" Judy asked. Mara nodded.

"It was pretty gross," Shoshanna said, and something popped into her head—the time Adam found a baby possum under the sink and cut its head off with a meat cleaver. She was glad Mara hadn't been around for that.

"I definitely draw the line at filth and vermin, but a kitchen should feel like a place where baking and cooking and eating happens," Judy said.

"Like your kitchen," Shoshanna said. "That was perfect."

Judy laughed. "Mine had everything plus the kitchen sink. Seriously, it was stacked floor to ceiling. Remember? And all those smells, like yeast and sprouts fermenting. You would not have believed some of the crazy stuff I came across when I packed up. I have to admit, though, I agree with you, Shosh. Culinary chaos, my friends used to call it. And yes, it was perfect."

Mara opened the refrigerator. "All he has in here is a lemon and half a stick of butter."

"Mara, I'm not sure you should be looking in there." Shoshanna reached over Mara's blond head to shut the door. "Anyway, there's not much to see."

"My guess is he must eat out a lot," Judy said. "When we get settled in the barn, we'll have to invite him over for a home-cooked dinner." She paused for a moment, tapping her fingers against the turquoise Formica counter. "Girls, I'm worried about your mother. She is totally bummed out. Is she always this tired?"

"She's up and down," Shoshanna said. "Sometimes she's fine, and she has energy and tells a lot of jokes. When we were planning our escape, she was full of energy. She could barely even sleep. But when she's worried, all she wants to do is sleep. She's worried about Adam and stuff. About him finding us."

"At Sweet Earth, they used to say she was checked out," Mara added.

"Checked out?" Judy asked.

Shoshanna explained, "It was like she was there but not there. Adam would get really mad and yell at her because she wasn't working in the orchard. He would try to make her go into his room with him and the others but she wouldn't."

Mara added, "Sometimes he used to hit her really hard, like he was trying to wake her up. That's how come we both lost our front tooth on the same day." She shrugged. "She didn't even cry."

Judy shook her head. "How long was that going on, Shoshie?"

"As long as I can remember," Shoshanna said. "Some days were better than others, though. The thing is, even when she was doing well, like when she had a lot of energy, Adam didn't like that either. He called her psycho. He said she was a crazy bitch. He used to tell me and Mara that if we turned out like her, he'd shoot us."

"That was just a joke, Shosh. He pointed his finger at us like it was a gun but it wasn't real. It was just pretend. It was just a joke," Mara said.

Judy murmured something under her breath, then looked at them. "Man, I'm so glad you guys left. It's funny, but now that I think of it, when you guys lived in San Francisco, your mother had a whole month when she didn't get out of bed and didn't talk to anyone. Not a word. Remember that?"

Shoshanna nodded. "That's when I went to the Free School and learned how to read and write. I would come home and tell her about it, and she'd just lay there with her eyes closed. Adam's friend Skye was nice about it, though. She got some books for me to read."

"Yeah. I remember Skye. She and your dad took off and went to Mexico for a month and left you guys with us. I forgot about that."

"Mom will start feeling better," Shoshanna said. "It just takes time. Then she'll be happy again. That's just how it goes. I think it's going to help, not having to deal with Adam."

"I'm sure you're right." Judy said. "Maybe a clean house will make her feel better even faster. What do you say we grab all of these things and start? Here, Shosh, you take the mop and bucket, and Mara, grab the sponges and paper towels. I've got the cleaning supplies."

They began washing down the kitchen because Judy told them it was the best place to start ("My mom always told me the kitchen is the heart and soul of a house," she told them) and also the biggest challenge. Shoshanna scrubbed out every drawer and every shelf, first with soap and water, then with bleach. It was hard work, but it was satisfying to watch the layer of black grime come off on her sponge and the surfaces turn from a mottled gray to their original white.

Judy cleaned the floor, first with the mop before finally giving up and going to Avery's house for a scrub brush.

She dumped soap and ammonia into the bucket, filled it with water, and scrubbed the entire expanse on her hands and knees. Mara was given demolition duty and got started enthusiastically tearing down the sagging wallpaper, which pulled off easily. Judy rolled the wallpaper up and carted it out to the garbage can by Avery's back door.

"When you're all finished, I'm going to scrub down those walls. Don't you think they would look great painted blue?"

"How about purple?" Shoshanna asked. "That's my favorite color."

"Yellow!" Mara chimed in. "I like yellow!"

"Why not a wall for each one of us?" Judy laughed. "We'll ask you mother what color she wants. That way we all get to express ourselves."

"I'm not sure that's gonna look good, but it's a cool idea," Shoshanna said.

"I bet Mom will say she doesn't care what color we paint her wall, and if we pester her about it, she'll pick gray," Mara said. Shoshanna hated to admit it, but she thought her sister was probably right.

CHAPTER FIVE

They had finished cleaning the kitchen and were crammed together working on the bathroom in the hallway between Ella's and Judy's rooms. It proved to be another revelation. On first inspection, with a sink full of empty fertilizer bags and a bathtub black with mildew, the girls thought it was one of the most disgusting bathrooms they'd ever seen—and they'd seen some pretty disgusting bathrooms.

"This might be one of the worst I've seen," Shoshanna said. "And that's pretty bad, considering the fact that we had to use a hundred-year-old outhouse at Sweet Earth Farm."

Judy laughed. "Apparently, Shosh, you've forgotten the bathroom on Clayton Street. The ferns and the clothesline were always hanging in the shower, along with the cheese in the cheesecloth dripping from the showerhead. Then this crazy dude named Nitro moved in and he liked to sleep in the tub. Not bathe in the tub, because he never bathed, just sleep in the tub. That place was foul." Shoshanna and Mara laughed.

After hours of energetic scrubbing, they could see that what they'd thought were clots of mold were actually tiny blue flowers on the tile. And with lots of bleach and sustained effort, the grout—which had been mildewed and gray—grudgingly turned off-white.

They'd thought the bathroom had no source of light, but the biggest surprise was discovering that a large sheet of plywood wasn't a makeshift wall patch but a covered window. When they pried it away with the claw end of Avery's ancient hammer, the plywood crashed to the floor and the afternoon sunlight streamed in. Judy started to sing "Let the Sun Shine In" as Shoshanna opened the window. Mara applauded.

"I wish we had a screen to keep out the bugs, but at least we have a window. I'll need you two to help me take this plywood outside. When the toilet arrives and is up and running, and when I get your toilet working, I think we're about ready to call this place home."

The girls picked up one end of the plywood while Judy grabbed the other, and they carried the plywood outside. "Let's just lean it against the barn for now, okay?"

When they turned around, Shoshanna saw a figure in

the distance, walking slowly along the edge of the yard next to the wire fence that ran beside the road. "Look," she said. "There's a man in the yard."

"Hey!" Judy waved at him, and he waved back. "Come on, girls. That's Avery. You've got to meet him. He's a trip. He's going to love you two."

Shoshanna was grateful to stop the cleaning frenzy. Her right arm and shoulder actually ached from all the scrubbing they'd been doing, and she'd breathed in so much ammonia and bleach that the back of her throat was sore.

The girls followed Judy across the lawn. "Look!" Mara said, her dirt-streaked face glowing as she tugged at Shoshanna's arm. "He's got a puppy."

In addition to the puppy, Avery Elliot had one of the kindest faces Shoshanna had ever seen. From decades in the sun, his skin looked weathered, like aged leather, but the lines in his face seemed to have formed around a lifetime of smiling. His build was slim, even scrawny, but his face was reassuringly full and his rounded, rosy cheeks were mapped by a complex network of tiny red blood vessels.

His eyes, deep-set under wildly thick, gray eyebrows, were an intense blue. The color of his eyes reminded Shoshanna of a sapphire her mother had shown her one day, set in a gaudy ring that had appeared in a box of jewelry Adam had mysteriously acquired. She remembered being mesmerized by the stone for what seemed like hours. Then she put it back in the box, which she looked for the next day, but it had disappeared as swiftly as it had come.

"You got a puppy!" yelled Mara, dancing with delight. "What's its name?"

"This is Laddie. Like Lassie the dog on the TV, but since he's a boy, it's Laddie."

Neither Shoshanna or Mara had any idea what he was talking about—a dog named Lassie on TV?—but Shoshanna immediately decided she liked Avery's gravelly but gentle voice, the big space between his two front teeth, and the way his eyes crinkled up and almost disappeared when he smiled.

"I'm Avery Elliot, but you can both just call me Avery. I already met Miss Judy here. And you two are…?"

"Shoshanna." Shoshanna bent down to pat Laddie. "Shoshanna Ebersole."

"That's quite a mouthful of a name."

"I know. People usually call me Shosh or Shoshie. And you can just forget the Ebersole part." *I try to*, she thought.

"Shoshie. I like that. That's what I'll call you. And who are you, little lady?"

"Mara. I'm six. Can I pet your dog too?"

"You sure can. Laddie would like nothing better than lots of affection. Six is a great age. Enjoy it, Mara, because you'll get old and decrepit like me soon enough. Anyway, it's nice to meet you ladies. Welcome to my farm. It means a lot to me, this place. I was hoping my son would want it to be his, but it doesn't seem that's going to be the case. Anyway, you've all been hard at work, I see from the looks of you. There was a pretty big mess in there, am I right? I haven't been inside in over a year, and truthfully, I was afraid to look. When Dave lived there he let it get pretty run-down. Judy, you weren't just whistling Dixie when you told me you weren't afraid of hard work."

"I like getting my hands and everything else dirty. I know that sounds kind of crazy but I really do. Of course, I have these two wonderful helpers. We love the place. You should come inside and see what we've done. It looks great. After the toilets are fixed—"

"Right! I went to Sears this morning and got you the parts you'll need. I'll come over and fix it now if you want. The plumber will be putting in the new toilet tomorrow, and if you wouldn't mind helping me fix the other one... I might need help. This stupid Parkinson's means my hands just aren't reliable anymore. It drives me crazy. I used to be so good with my hands. Anyway, I had the electricity turned on this morning too. No phone service yet, but there's a phone jack somewhere that Dave put in when he started up the seed business. I can get that going for you if you like. Of course, you'd have to handle the monthly bill."

"We're not phone people, Avery. I think we can live without that."

Shoshanna knew her mother would never agree to a phone or anything Adam could use to track them down. *Maybe someday*, she thought. She remembered an ad for a phone shaped like a soda can in the *Seventeen* magazine she'd read at Jim and Francine's. She imagined having friends to call, or parties she'd get invited to. That would be fun.

"Now, didn't you tell me these girls have a mom?"

"Well, yes, she's inside…" Judy began.

"She's got the flu," the girls said in unison.

"The flu?" Avery scratched his head. "Wow. That's pretty rare, to get the flu in the late springtime."

"In Oregon you can get it any time of the year," Shoshanna told him. "Everyone at the commune was always getting it. Don't worry, she's okay. She just needs to rest."

"Well, I'm glad to hear that. I look forward to meeting her when she's feeling better. Listen, hang on for a sec. You stay here and entertain Laddie while I get the toilet innards out of the truck. I got you guys some groceries and stuff, just some staples. There's some flour and sugar and milk and coffee."

"Do you need a hand?" Shoshanna asked.

"I'll be okay, I think, but believe me, I'm not shy. I'll holler if I do." With that, he walked off. At first, Laddie was happy to enjoy the attention showered upon him by the girls, but when he saw Avery leave, he followed him, tail wagging.

"What a nice man," Mara said. "I was worried he'd be sick and grouchy since he has that shaking sickness. He's really cheerful, though."

"I don't think he feels well a lot of the time, but you'd never know it," Judy said.

"I'm really happy we can help him out. It's a good situation for all of us," Shoshanna added.

"I like Laddie too," Mara said. "Do you think he would let Laddie stay at our place?"

"I bet he'd like that," Shoshanna said. "At least, for visits." She smiled at her sister.

"Shosh," Judy asked, "I just wondered, where did you two come up with that story about the flu? It sounded to me like you guys rehearsed it."

"Melaya. Melaya was my mother's friend at Sweet Earth. She told me flu was the best excuse if you needed to be alone. Like, if the people at the commune wanted my mom to do things and she couldn't, or if Adam's friends tried to bother her when they were after him for money or dope, or if Adam was pestering her about paying attention to him. Sometimes she couldn't deal with it, so she told us to tell people she was dead. We didn't want to say that, so Melaya told us just to say she had the flu."

Judy shook her head and sighed. "I wish she felt better. I wish I knew a way to help her through this, short of erasing everything she's been through."

"You are helping her," Mara said. "You're helping her by taking care of us."

Mara's opinion about Judy's help didn't seem to be the case; at least not from the way Ella acted when they got back to the barn. She was up and pacing her bedroom floor. "Where have you all been?" she asked, her voice petulant. "I was calling for you. I hate being left here all alone."

"We were just out in the yard," Shoshanna said. "Sorry if you were worried—"

"I wasn't worried about you," Ella interrupted. "I'm out of cigarettes."

Shoshanna almost lashed back at Ella. But she softened when she saw just how nervous and fragile Ella seemed. "Yeah, well, sorry, but we have no money and no car. Plus, the nearest store is miles away."

"What the hell am I supposed to do, then?" Ella said, glaring at Shoshanna and then at Judy. "How did I get talked into this? Who decided we'd end up in the middle of stinking nowhere?"

"Wow." Shoshanna exhaled. She knew her mother was struggling, but her own frustration was quickly exceeding her sympathy. "Calm down, Ma. A lot of people have bent over backward for you, including me and Mara, and Judy most of all. Avery, who you haven't even met yet. You're acting like a spoiled brat!"

Ella didn't get angry. Instead she turned to Shoshanna with a childlike look on her face. "I know, I know. But, Shoshie, could you please go to the store and lift a pack of cigarettes? Please? It's the last time I'll ask, I promise. Five miles isn't that far. Maybe you can hitch a ride."

"I don't even know where a store is, Ma. And I'm done lifting anything." Shoshanna's voice had turned hard.

Ella glared at them. "Fine. Then you can all just go screw yourselves. You heard me. Get out and leave me the hell alone." She slammed the door to her room shut.

"Please tell me she doesn't get in moods like this often," Judy said.

"Just sometimes," Shoshanna said. "Not all the time. A lot of the time she's okay. She'll get over it. Part of it is wanting a cigarette."

"Once she cut off all my hair when she was in a bad mood," Mara said quietly. "With a razor."

"That was two years ago," Shoshanna said. "You had lice. It grew back."

"Once she forgot us. She drove us to Corvallis to meet that man and she forgot about us. We had to sleep on a bench outside. It was raining."

Shoshanna touched Mara on the arm gently. "Mara, you're only talking about the bad things. There were good times too. Remember those." Shoshanna could see tears in Mara's eyes. Mara started to cry.

"Hello? Anybody home?" Avery was standing at the front door.

"Be there in a sec!" Judy called, trying to sound cheerful.

Shoshanna knelt down next to her sister and said in almost a whisper, "Listen, Mara. Mom is a good mother. I've seen her take care of you and I know how kind and caring she is, and how much she loves you. She loves you so much. Right now she needs for all of us to stick together. So we need to be kind to Mom right now. Okay?" Mara nodded but kept her eyes cast downward.

"Come on. Let's see what Avery brought for dinner." Shoshanna led Mara toward the front of the house.

Avery was on the front steps, holding two large paper

grocery bags. "This is just part of it. I have four more bags in my pickup."

"Thanks, Avery! You are so kind." Judy smiled at Avery, and Avery's face lit up.

"Come on, Mara. If we each take a bag, we can get everything in one trip." Shoshanna tapped Mara's shoulder as she said this. Mara's tears stopped and she nodded. "Avery, you wait here. There's a chair in the corner. We'll be right back."

The three walked out to unload the bags from the back of the ancient, battered blue Ford pickup and carried them into the kitchen.

Shoshanna looked around her at the sun on the grass, the bags of food, the sound of Laddie barking at the back door. "We are so lucky," she announced to Judy, to Mara, to the universe. This may not have been the Plan, but in many ways, it was better. Best of all, it was real.

They got back to the kitchen to find Avery standing there, looking around approvingly. "Ladies, this place looks like you could eat off the floor. When Dave lived here, I don't think he cleaned it once, not once, and that no-good floozy he was with definitely didn't lift a finger, except to eat bonbons in front of her soap operas." He pointed to the bags. "I think I got enough stuff. I wasn't sure what your taste was, so I got a bunch of everything. You girls like Frosted Flakes?"

"We never had them," Mara told him.

"Nothing beats Tony the Tiger." Avery pointed to the grinning cartoon tiger on the box. "See? Tony says, 'They're grrrrreat!' I got you some chicken for dinner. I hope that's okay."

Shoshanna and Mara thought of meat as a rare treat. The Sweet Earth Farm members liked to tell people they were vegetarians, but the truth was, they didn't eat meat because it was almost never an option. When the commune got a good deal on chicken from a nearby poultry farm one time, they ate chicken for a month. When one of the cows died, they ate beef. They were not vegetarians. They were opportunists and sometimes just plain scavengers.

"Thank you, Avery. You really got us everything we could possibly ask for and more. We are set for a while." Shoshanna smiled.

"If I forgot anything, you just let me know. And now, it's about time for my daily siesta." With that, he walked toward the door.

"Would you like to eat dinner with us?" Judy called after him. "I hope you don't think I'm nosy, but your refrigerator looked pretty empty when we were over this morning."

"I peeked," Mara said. "I saw the lemon."

Avery laughed. "Yes, well, I'm not much of a cook.

I generally have supper at the Half Moon Diner. They make good pies, and the meat loaf's not half bad. It's got to the point where they kind of expect me every night."

"How about a home-cooked meal?" Shoshanna asked. "Come on, Avery. Look at all this wonderful stuff you got us. What do you say? Chicken, mashed potatoes, corn on the cob…"

"Hell, if you have baking powder, I could even make biscuits," Judy added.

Avery shrugged. "Well, I don't know…"

"You could bring Laddie," Mara said, tugging at his sleeve. "Please?"

"It would be fun," Shoshanna added.

Avery grinned. "In that case, we'd be delighted."

"Great. Be back by six, okay?"

"Yes, ma'am."

They set to work. Much to everyone's relief, the old stove worked, and there were even enough pots and pans and dishes for every purpose and every person. There were makeshift elements to the presentation (what things got cooked in was what they got served in, they used paper towels instead of napkins, and no two place settings even remotely matched), but when Avery walked in the door, a complete meal was on the table, down to daisies picked from the yard and candles, balanced precariously in juice glasses, that had been relocated from Judy's apartment.

"This is not only a treat for the eyes, but for the taste buds too," Avery proclaimed, taking a bite of chicken. "Mmm. Just like my wife used to make. And I'm not just being polite. One thing you'll find out about me, I value truth more than politeness."

"Then we should get along just fine," Shoshanna told him, passing him another biscuit. "We are all honest too. Almost to a fault." She winked at Mara.

"And here's another honest statement," Judy chimed in. "I think this arrangement is going to work out really well."

"We love it here," Mara said. "We love you. And Laddie. And the TV."

Over dinner, Avery told them about how he'd made an investment in the stock market when he was in his twenties. He'd put his money in Pacific Gas and Electric, which turned out to be a wise decision. With the six-hundred-fifty-dollar profit he made after selling his shares, he decided to buy some land. He'd grown up in Fresno, which was in California's Central Valley. The area was prone to both floods and drought, and it was racked by a dusty desert breeze. The Pacific, cut off by the mountains, could have been on another planet.

"It was kinda like living in a blast furnace. One day, I just got it in my head to take a ride out to the ocean. I fell in love with Half Moon Bay like some guys fall for a gal," Avery told them. "I was smitten. I moved lock, stock, and barrel without a second thought. And that wasn't a typical thing for me, no, sir. I've always been a deliberate sort of person, so it was definitely out of character."

"So you just found this house, and that was that?" Judy asked.

"No, I just found this piece of property. I built the house myself thirty-seven years ago, in 1936. It's funny. I ordered the blueprint from a Sears catalog. It was your basic ranch house, and that suited me just fine, being a bachelor and all. We added the dormers later, after Dave was born. I didn't want anything fancy, just a roof over my head. I really felt that the land was home. I could walk out into my yard and smell the ocean. The barn was already here. That means that your house is way older than my house. In fact, there was a little shack of a house right where I built my own, but it was just in bad shape so I tore it down.

"The barn was in good condition, though, so I left it standing. Then I bought some used farm equipment, a tractor and a thresher. Everyone around here planted beans and artichokes, so I figured that's what the soil was good for. That was about right. Seventy acres, and that first year I planted over forty. I had a bunch of seasonal guys from Baja helping me out the first few years, which was a good thing, because even though I studied up on it in the off-season, I still didn't know what the hell I was doing. Do you mind if I smoke?"

"Not at all," Judy said.

"Hey, could my mom have a cigarette?" asked Mara. "She wanted one real bad before and we didn't know how to get her any."

"That's impolite, Mara," Shoshanna said. "That's okay, Avery. Don't feel obligated."

"No, honey, I don't mind. Hey, here, Mara, take the pack. Tell her it's from one smoker to another. I hope I'll get to meet her soon."

"Thanks!" Mara ran off to the bedroom.

"What happened then? After you'd been farming for a while?"

"Well, I'd been living here for a few years, just trying to keep my head above water. I didn't do much besides work the farm, eat, and sleep. Then Carl, a buddy of mine who runs the five-and-dime in town, had a party out at his place, a New Year's Eve bash. I don't go in for parties much, but I figured, what the hell, New Year's is New Year's, right? It's not like I had anything going on.

"Anyway, he invited this woman who was new in town. She was a teacher over at the elementary school, real smart gal. Name was Margaret O'Brien. Black Irish, you know, with dark hair and green eyes. Well, that was it for me. Six months later, we got married, and nine months after that to the day, we had Dave."

"Where is your wife now?" Shoshanna asked.

"She passed away, Shosh," Judy said, sending her a gaze that said, *Careful, touchy subject.*

"I'm sorry," Shoshanna said.

"Not a day goes by that I don't miss her," Avery said, putting down his fork and looking out the window. "She'll be gone six years this September, and I still can't get used to it. Sometimes I turn around and expect to see her, or I start to ask her a question or tell her a joke. Then I remember."

Mara came bounding back into the kitchen. "My mom says thank you so much."

"Actually, I had to come out and thank you in person," Ella said, leaning against the doorjamb, cigarette in her hand. "Also, I needed a light."

"Avery, this is Ella. Mom, this is Avery." Shoshanna introduced them.

Avery held out his hand and Ella shook it. "I hope you're feeling better. Your kids tell me you got the flu."

Without missing a beat, Ella replied, "Yeah. Thanks. I guess I caught some bug up in Oregon. It's still winter up there, you know. Spring comes late. It's got me feeling really tired. Plus, I'm surrounded by these nonsmokers who don't realize the life-and-death importance of a cigarette."

"Well, we've just got to take care of each other, then." Avery smiled. "Here, have a light."

Ella sat down next to Avery, cigarette in her mouth, and leaned forward while he lit it. She'd changed out of the old tie-dyed T-shirt she'd been wearing for the past few days, and had put on a pair of men's overalls and a white gauze top. She'd even brushed her hair. She looked thin but downright pretty. Shoshanna looked over at Mara and smiled. Mara smiled back. *Maybe*, Shoshanna thought, *this was when things would start to get better again.*

That night, Shoshanna and Mara lay on their bed wrapped in a nest of blankets, heads resting deep in the down pillows Jim and Francine had given them, listening drowsily to the quiet voices of Ella and Judy sitting at the kitchen table. They could hear their plan to get up early the next day and start on the painting and repair of the roadside stand. Ella's voice sounded strong, clear, and definite, like she'd finally woken up and decided to pull her weight, though Shoshanna knew from experience that things might be different in the morning. But still, their quiet conversation sounded hopeful, interspersed with laughter.

Mara started whispering to Shoshanna about how

much she loved Avery, Laddie, and Frosted Flakes. "I love it here. Even more than San Francisco. I didn't have a TV or dog until today, and now I do. There are good vibes here, Shoshie, doncha think?"

"Yep," Shoshanna replied, yawning. "Real good vibes, Mara. Now go to sleep."

After Mara's breathing deepened, Shoshanna listened to the distant hum of the highway. Every few minutes a car or truck would rumble by, the engine growing louder, then softer as it drove away. She wondered if she'd ever stop worrying about the possibility of a time that one car would not keep going but turn up the dirt driveway, pull up to the barn, cut the engine, and dim the lights.

The driver's side door would open, and a man would get out. Adam. He'd be holding a gun or a meat cleaver or a knife or a baseball bat—any of the things she'd seen him use to threaten or hurt or even kill. She wished she could control the way her thoughts worked, turning from her hopeful future to her terrifying past.

Gradually, she was able to shut the bad thoughts out, to attach her mind to the soft laughter in the kitchen, Mara's regular breathing, and the distant hum of cars. She heard Laddie bark and imagined Avery turning out his porch light. He was smiling. That was enough for her to let go of her nightmare visions and slide into sleep.

CHAPTER SIX

Honey, you need a man to give you a hand with that?" A man wearing a cowboy hat and driving a battered pickup truck leaned out of his window.

"No thanks," Shoshanna said, holding up the sign she'd painted for the vegetable stand.

"Are you sure, darlin'? I'd love to help you out in any way I can, and I mean, any way."

"I said no." Shoshanna looked him square in the eyes as she said this.

"She's fine," Judy yelled, adding, "her only problem is idiots like you."

The man yelled an obscenity and drove off in a cloud of dust.

Ella had no reaction to what she'd seen and heard other than saying, "It's going to be tough to get that sign to hang even."

"Thanks for helping me get rid of that jerk," Shoshanna said quietly to Judy.

"No problem, Shosh. You're going to need that skill in your life. You are a beautiful girl."

Shoshanna was always surprised when people told her that—and they'd been saying it more and more often lately. More than anything, the comment made her uncomfortable. When she looked in the mirror, she just saw her father. It was hard—impossible, really—for her to see the beauty in that.

"How did you learn to deal with these redneck guys?" Shoshanna asked. "They must always be flirting with you."

Judy shrugged. "Practice. I think of them as being like stray dogs. If you yell at them, then ignore them, they start sniffing around somewhere else."

Ella looked grim. "At Sweet Earth, it was never that simple. They wouldn't take no for an answer."

"All I can do is thank God you're not there anymore," Judy said softly. "You or your daughters."

"Maybe the sign should go on the bottom," Shoshanna suggested. "I know it's not as visible from the road, but if we hang it on the top, it'll hit us on the head every time we have to lean over the counter. What do you think, Judy?"

"Okay. Let me get the hammer. Shoshie, where's Mara?"

"She was helping me sand the wood, but then she had to pee and now she's picking flowers and playing with Laddie," Shoshanna replied.

Ella looked exasperated. Judy laughed. "Aw, El, just let her be a kid. She's only six. What were you accomplishing when you were six?"

They kept working through the morning. Shoshanna was happy with the way the stand was turning out. When she first saw it, she'd believed her mother's assessment that it was a lost cause. After whitewashing the whole structure, Shoshanna, Judy, and Mara painted flowers along the front in bright primary colors. Then Judy got concerned that people driving by would think they sold flowers rather than vegetables. So, since Shoshanna was good at lettering, she made a sign that said Farm Fresh Produce. They'd sanded the wood around the doors and windows and were waiting for the morning fog to lift before painting the trim avocado green.

"Whoa, baby! You with the legs! Dump the hippies and come work at my place!" a man in a pickup hollered.

"Stupid ass," Ella muttered.

"I'll say." Judy climbed down from the ladder, ready to fight.

But Shoshanna was the first to fire back. "What's wrong with you, pervert?" she yelled at the pickup driver.

"Try hitting on some bimbo closer to your own age."

The pickup drove off in a cloud of dust and Judy smiled proudly at Shoshanna. A familiar truck came down the road, slowly.

"Thank God. Talk about a good man being hard to find. At last one has arrived. It's Avery with lunch," Judy said.

"Yay! I'm starving," Mara said, running in from the field with flowers in her hand and Laddie right behind her.

"You're always starving," Ella said. She had been in a bad mood all day.

Shoshanna ignored her comment and tried to lighten her mother's mood. "Come on, Ma. Stop and eat. Look at you. You're skin and bones, and you can barely lift the paintbrush. I swear, you're living on cigarettes and coffee."

Avery got out of the truck slowly and, holding on to the door, shook his head. "My God, girls, what have you done?" For a moment, Shoshanna's heart sank, then she saw that he was grinning. "I won't be able to keep the customers away."

"What do you think?" Judy asked. "We were trying to make it look cheerful."

"Cheerful is an understatement."

"Wait'll you see the green we picked for the trim. It's the same color as an avocado."

"Didn't they have any artichoke green or green-bean

green at the store?" Avery teased. "I brought you gals some takeout from the diner. I didn't know what you liked so I just guessed. There's grilled cheese and tuna and good, old-fashioned peanut butter and jelly. Mara, there's a little treat in there for you. For you too, Ella, even though I know that nasty habit will be the death of us."

Shoshanna watched her mother's face light up and thought for a moment how nice it would be if she could make Ella that happy—if only she could make her as happy as nicotine did. But addiction is powerful. She'd seen enough of that at Sweet Earth.

Mara started tugging at the bag to see what Avery had brought. "Coca-Cola in little bottles!" she shrieked.

After they'd finished their sodas and sandwiches, Mara examined Avery's treat: a box of chocolate cookies with a layer of white cream in the middle.

"What're these?" Mara asked.

"Oreos! You girls are about to discover yet another classic American taste sensation," Judy said. She then proceeded to show them what she maintained was the best way to eat an Oreo, unscrewing the top and scraping the layer of cream off with her teeth, then eating the chocolate cookie separately.

After eating, they set back to work, painting the window and door trim. Judy was tall enough to reach the top of the door frame without a ladder, while Ella stood on the ladder, painting the top of the windows and Shoshanna and Mara painted the bottom.

After a while, Ella stepped back to look at their progress. "You have to be careful of clumps and drips. Shosh, you missed a spot. Right under the windowsill, see? Mara, that's way too much paint on your brush. It's dripping all over the ground. Careful, you're about to step in it. We'll never have enough to cover everything at the rate you're wasting it."

Funny, Shoshanna thought, most people hate criticism, but coming from Ella, it felt good. It felt like she cared. It felt like all this—the shed, the farm, everything— mattered to her.

Within an hour, they were done. They all stepped back. No one said anything. Then, Shoshanna shook her head. "The green looked better in the can," she said. "It looks kind of icky. It's too dark, maybe, or too dull. It doesn't match the flowers that Mara and I did."

"Yeah." Judy nodded. "I see what you mean. It doesn't match, but still, it's better than it was. It's certainly unique. No one's going to be able to ignore it. Maybe it'll grow on us. I can't think of anything else in the world that's painted this color."

"You're right," Ella said. "And there's probably a reason for that. But what's done is done. I guess we'd better clean up."

"I think it's pretty," said Mara.

"That makes one of us," Shoshanna said and then gave Mara a hug. "Never mind. I'm only teasing. It really is better than it was."

That night they fell into bed, exhausted. Mara was asleep as soon as her head hit the pillow. Shoshanna's painting arm ached, and her shoulders were sunburned. As tired as she was, she couldn't fall asleep right away. She was still awake when Ella came in.

"Squeeze over, Shosh. Do you mind?"

"Not at all."

Shoshanna felt Ella touch her arm and then she whispered, "You know what? You two, you girls, I did right. Adam was my biggest mistake, but then I think, without him, I wouldn't have you guys. And the crazy thing is, even knowing all the shit he'd put me through, all the messed-up stuff, I'd do it again if it meant bringing you and Mara into the world."

"I love you, Ma." Shoshanna felt tears sting her eyes.

"And I love you, Shosh. Thanks for letting me crash with you guys tonight. It's calming me down."

Shoshanna woke up to the sound of her mother coughing and the squeak of the mattress springs as she turned over. Shoshanna pulled the blanket up under her chin and moved farther away from Mara's dirty feet and jagged toenails. She was drifting toward sleep again when she saw her mother sit up quietly and ease herself out of the bed.

She watched as Ella grabbed a flannel shirt and went out into the kitchen. More coughing, and the sound of water running from the faucet. Then, she heard the front door close.

Shoshanna jumped out of bed to see if her nightmare had come true—a car waiting in the shadows with Oregon plates. But there was nothing, just the clear night sky and the sound of crickets chirping. She went back to lie in the warm softness of the bed for several seconds, waiting to see if Ella would just come back inside. Finally, heaving a sigh, she rolled out of the warm blankets and pulled on a sweatshirt. She knew her mother was getting emotionally stronger, but she also knew she was far from okay. When she was like this—depressed and agitated—she needed to be watched.

As Shoshanna walked toward the front door, her heart started pounding and she thought about a sunny spring morning a couple of years before, when she was twelve. She'd followed her mother out to the toolshed to ask if she could take Mara down to the brook to catch tadpoles. It was after a very dark time that had lasted almost the entire winter, but with the warm weather, Ella seemed to be getting better. In fact, she had been oddly cheerful all morning.

Shoshanna knew her mother well enough to temper her relief with skepticism. She had a feeling that something was not quite right. When she walked in through the open shed door, she was just in time to see Ella slice through her left wrist with a hacksaw. She'd already cut her right wrist, and blood was everywhere. It dripped off her arms in what looked to Shoshanna like two red rivers and had begun to pool on the thick-planked wooden floor.

Shoshanna screamed, and the women who had been hanging laundry on the clothesline sauntered over. A group of people had been smoking hash on the back steps, and they drifted over too, but didn't do anything. They just stood by, looking confused and saying things like "Oh man" and "Where's Adam?" Reality suddenly set in when Ella collapsed. People began to panic, shouting out contradictory directions on how to stop the bleeding. One of the men who was particularly stoned tried to subdue Ella, who was screaming for everyone to leave her alone and let her die, by lying on top of her.

Celia, the only woman at Sweet Earth with any common sense, started making tourniquets out of T-shirts from the clothesline and yelled at Shoshanna to find Adam.

She did find Adam…on top of Melaya in the bedroom with all the shades pulled down. They were both naked and twisting around and making terrible moaning noises. She screamed at him to come quick, that Ella had hurt herself and she was dying. And he threw his work boot at her and told her to get the hell out—couldn't she see he was busy?

In the meantime, Celia got into the car and drove down the road to the nearest house and called an ambulance. Ella was loaded onto a stretcher with her homemade tourniquets and rushed to the hospital. Shoshie held Mara, who wouldn't stop crying. Adam later refused to pay the bill.

But of all these terrible things, the thing that made Shoshanna feel sick every time she thought about that day was that when she had first walked in and saw the cutting and the blood, Ella had looked over at her and smiled. As bad as everything else had been, at least it all made some kind of awful sense. The smile was terrifying. The smile was the thing she didn't understand.

The smile was the reason she didn't want to ever leave her mother alone when she was going through a bad time. And even though Ella got out of the hospital and vowed that she would never try to end her life again, that she'd had a revelation as the life was draining from her body that her job here was not yet done, Shoshanna still worried.

Walking outside, Shoshanna looked around. She didn't see Ella anywhere, but she was afraid to call her name. She felt her throat catch and she swallowed back a sob as she began to run toward the road. As she neared Avery's house, she noticed that the back porch light was on. In the shadows, out near Laddie's doghouse, she could see a shape hunched over the old wooden picnic table. She saw the red glow of a cigarette, and she knew it was Ella. She felt a wave of relief wash over her. She took a deep breath and walked over.

"Ma?"

"Yeah?" Ella sounded tired but calm.

Shoshanna didn't want to ask if she was okay. She knew her mother hated that question. Shoshanna also knew that whatever had broken in her mother had been put back together, but the cracks were still there and could split open with prying. She had learned to talk softly, not touch unless Ella touched her first, and not intrude.

"What are you doing up? You should be sleeping. You've had a long day."

"So have you." Shoshanna sat on the grass, which was browned out, sharp, and dry. It scratched the backs of her legs. "I couldn't fall asleep."

"Join the club." Ella took a long drag and exhaled. Shoshanna looked up at the stars. The sky was a sea of them. A lone car passed on the road. It only had one headlight. "You know, I've been thinking."

"About what?" Shoshanna reached over to snuff out the glowing cigarette butt her mother had tossed.

"I like it here. I like being in the country. I like Avery. He's a cool old dude. I like the barn."

"That's good, Ma. I like everything too. So does Judy. So does Mara."

Ella sighed. "What I'm thinking is I like it, but it can't last."

Shoshanna felt her stomach lurch. "Why not?"

"'Cause the stuff you like doesn't last. That's life. You feel good, you're happy, and one day everything changes and suddenly it's all shit again. You try to hold on to it, and that makes it worse. Desperate. It all turns to shit in the end. That's life. I hate to say it, but mark my words."

"No, Ma," Shoshanna said. "Not always. Sometimes that's true, but sometimes things get better and stay better. Sometimes people get to be happy."

Ella got up and stretched. "Man, my throat feels like crap. I can't seem to kick this cough. Come on, Shosh. We gotta get some sleep. We have a lot of stuff to do tomorrow—Judy said we'll be going from sunup to sundown. Even if we can't sleep, we've got to rest."

"Okay." They walked back to the barn.

Ella laughed. "Remember that night we camped out near the river? That was wild."

"Yeah." Shoshanna couldn't help but grin. "I was so scared. I thought every noise was a bear. Then the dog woke me up and I thought she was a bear."

"Uh-huh. And then I yelled at you to quit being such a baby because there were no bears where we were. Then when we saw the bear going through our bag of supplies, you thought it was a dog and started running over to play with it. God. I don't even remember how we got up that tree. And I had Mara strapped to me in the front pack screaming bloody murder.

"That dumb bear had us treed for, what? Like, hours. I tried to keep you calm by telling you stories even though I was totally freaking out. Man, that was crazy." She draped her arm around Shoshanna's shoulder, but Shoshanna didn't try to settle in. She just accepted the weight.

CHAPTER SEVEN

It had been a solid week of fog, lifting only late in the day, late enough to catch the faint pink and peach of the setting sun as the day faded into nightfall. Then they would go to sleep to wake once again to gray. The grass around the house and barn had gone from light green to gold to brown, because even though the clouds were a constant, no rain fell.

Avery had an irrigation system for the artichokes and beans. It would turn on at six thirty every morning and snap off at seven, then go on again from five until six in the afternoon. Shoshanna woke every morning to the click, whir, chop, chop, chop, chop of the sprinklers. She loved hearing the sound, loved the way it underlined her first waking thought: *I'm here, still here, in Half Moon Bay*.

Working in the field was tiring, but Shoshanna didn't mind. She liked picking the artichokes best, because they fit almost perfectly into the palm of her hand, and because there was a yank, twist, and snap method to picking that even Avery told her she was good at. A natural, he called her, and it made her glow with pride. Then there were the beans. The beans seemed endless. They were rough, scratchy against her fingertips, and she was grateful when her calluses toughened up. Weeding was the worst. The dirt, more black than brown, would work its way under her fingernails, and her back and neck ached from being hunched over. They all worked in a line, Judy, Ella, her, and Mara.

Fred and Dixon, two men Avery hired every year to help with the picking, worked the fields too. They lived in an old green trailer parked at the edge of Avery's field, and when it wasn't harvest time, they had a small boat down at the marina and they fished out in the bay. Fred and Dixon were old, even older than Avery, and they weren't much for talking. They set their row up on the other side of the field from the women to avoid conversation.

Time had a rhythm. After breakfast, the four of them would go out and wave at Fred and Dixon, who would wave back. Then they set to work. The six of them—sometimes Avery would join in if he felt up to it—would then pick steadily until noon. Then, after lunch, Judy, Ella, and the girls would work at the stand until five, while

Fred and Dixon packed the vegetables they'd picked that morning into wooden crates and loaded them onto the pickup truck to take to the grocery store.

At the stand, Judy and Ella would talk to the customers, take the money, and make the change. Shoshanna would weigh the vegetables and Mara would bag them. Sometimes people gave the girls candy or spare change. Mara especially loved the attention. "We're quite a team, aren't we?" Judy liked to say, and Shoshanna would agree.

For the first time in her life, days had steadiness, predictability. People with conventional jobs would come by the stand and talk about how they hated the drudgery of their daily routine, but for Shoshanna and Mara, the farming life they had fallen into was wonderful for its security. Even better than feeling happy, they felt content.

One afternoon, a car pulled up to the stand, and Ella froze. A man and woman got out and walked over. Shoshanna was in the back, rearranging some bins of artichokes, when the two came up to the stand.

"Hello, can I help you?" Shoshanna had seen her mother's reaction and ran behind the counter. "Indigo?" she said. "Is that you?"

"Oh my God," the woman said. "Adam's kid, right? What are you doing down here?" Indigo looked at Ella and showed no sign of recognizing her, probably because the Ella she knew never got out of bed, never even showed her face.

"We moved," Shoshanna said, feeling the heat of her mother's gaze. She knew to keep things vague. For all they knew, Indigo might be communicating with Adam.

"Where's your dad?" Indigo asked. "I haven't seen him in years. This is my old man, Otto." Unsmiling, Otto nodded at them and started looking over the beans and artichokes.

"Hi," Judy broke in. "I'm Judy, a neighbor of theirs."

"I'm Elaine. Well, the girls know me as Indigo, but I went back to my real name when I left Sweet Earth a few years ago. Man, that scene was messed up. I'm actually really glad to see that you're still alive. Adam almost killed me, spiritually and physically." She lifted her hair to reveal a scar at the base of her neck. "He didn't like it when I said no. I heard he got into a lot of trouble after I split."

"Yeah, it's true," Judy said. "We haven't seen him either."

Ella's eyes went wild with fear. Shoshanna tried to give her mother a knowing glance, but Ella seemed to be off in her own world.

"Count your blessings," Elaine-Indigo said. "I know I do every day. We'll take these artichokes." She handed Judy a five-dollar bill. "Keep the change. And Shoshanna—listen, remember that thing I said to you about the black hole in your heart..." Shoshie nodded. "I was talking about your dad. Not you. You're going to be okay."

"That was scary," Ella said after Elaine and Otto drove off. "I don't know. I feel like I'm never going to shake Adam. In little ways, he keeps resurfacing. I'm just waiting for him to show up one day. He will too. It's a matter of time."

"I'm telling you, Ma, we've landed in a safe place. He's not going to find us." Shoshanna tried to sound convincing, even though she was worried too.

Judy added, "Your past sends out little scouts to keep finding you, like this Indigo chick, but Adam's not going to risk getting arrested to track you down."

"You don't know Adam," Ella said and went back to sorting beans. Shoshanna hated to admit it, but she knew her mother was right.

✳ ✳ ✳

As time went on, Judy would sometimes question, rather wistfully, if she'd ever have time to do anything creative or artistic again. Ella put up a good front for the customers but privately complained about the relentlessness of the early-to-bed, early-to-rise routine, because some days she was tired and would love to sleep in an extra half hour, or some days she didn't feel like making small talk, and some days her back hurt and she didn't feel like bending over to pick beans or artichokes. There were even a few days that she begged off work entirely, pleading a headache or cramps.

Judy, Shoshanna, and Mara would go out and work without her, and when they got home, she was always up and about, watching television or smoking a cigarette at the picnic table in the yard. Shoshanna knew by the set of her jaw that this annoyed Judy, but Judy said nothing.

One day when Fred and Dixon made a comment about Ella's sick days, Judy was quick to defend her. "Hey, guys, you don't know what's she's been through. You don't have a freakin' clue. It's a miracle she's still alive and that Shosh and Mara are okay. She's responsible for getting them out to safety. She needs to heal. It's gonna take her a little time to get into the swing of this."

"Yeah," Fred grumbled. "We all pull our weight, though. She don't."

"She does too. In fact, she's pulled more weight alone in the past few years than you two dudes could handle together in ten lifetimes," Judy replied.

Fred mumbled something and walked off. "Fred is mean," Mara said.

Shoshanna appreciated Judy's dedication to her mother since Shoshanna often agreed with Fred and Dixon. "He's just grouchy today, Mare," Shoshanna said.

"He has arthritis, that's what Avery told me, and his joints ache when it's damp out. It's pretty damp today."

At lunchtime, Mara dripped grape jelly all over the front of her shirt and Shoshanna went home to get her a new one before going to the stand. When she walked into the kitchen, she heard Ella coughing, then saw her snuff out her cigarette and begin pacing back and forth, from the sink to the stove to the refrigerator, like an animal in a pen.

"Are you feeling better, Ma?"

"A little." She paused to toss the cigarette butt into the trash can. "Not up to working, though."

"Maybe tomorrow," Shoshanna said, exhaling sharply, summoning her patience.

"Yeah. Definitely tomorrow." Shoshanna turned to leave. "Wait, Shosh. I've been thinking…what do you think about moving back to San Francisco? I don't think farming is my thing." Suddenly Ella started coughing. She leaned over the sink and spit into it. Shoshanna saw that the wad of spit in the white porcelain sink was bloody.

"Ma, you're bleeding."

"Yeah, I know. It's no big deal. Just a cough. My throat is dry. Seriously, though, what do you think of going back to the city? You guys liked it there."

"I don't want to leave. I like it here. I love Judy. Avery is so nice to us."

Ella sighed. "Yeah, I know." She leaned over the counter and looked out the window at the clothes on the line and the acres of plants stretching into the distance. "But don't you think it gets boring, being around the same people in the same place, doing the same thing, day in and day out?"

"No. It's never exactly the same. And even when I'm doing stuff I've done before, I don't mind."

Ella snorted derisively. "It's boring, Shosh. That's what it is."

Shoshanna's grasp on her patience slipped. She looked at her mother. "Think about it, Ma. I've lived with beatings and threats, no food in the house, drugs, drug overdoses, shoplifting, and wearing the same clothes for a month straight. Your suicide attempt. My father is apparently a murderer. Bored? For once, I don't wake up scared because I can't even imagine what terrible thing is going to happen next."

Ella drew her hand back and slapped Shoshanna across the face with surprising force. "Well, that's your trip. I hate to say it, and it's a bummer for you, but you and Mara are my kids, and the three of us are gonna have to split if I want to."

Shoshanna cradled her cheek in her hand, tears springing to her eyes. "What do you mean?"

"Split, Shosh. Leave. I'm thinking of packing you two up and getting the hell out of here."

"I have to get back to the stand, Ma. It's the busy time of day, and Judy and Mara are out there alone." She ran out, slamming the screen door behind her. She felt suddenly nauseous. How could her mother do this to them? She'd taken forever to leave Sweet Earth Farm, and now that they'd finally found somewhere nice to live, she'd quickly decided to move on? Couldn't she see they were happy for the first time ever?

Shoshanna decided she wouldn't tell Mara because she didn't want her to worry. Moving would break Mara's heart. It was breaking Shoshanna's heart. Her head was spinning by the time she got back to the stand.

"You okay, Shosh?" Judy asked. "You look upset."

"Yeah. My stomach hurts a little." This was, in fact, true.

"Join the club. Man, too many potato chips. I might have to tell Avery to quit bringing us those. I think I ate half a bag by myself."

Shoshanna tried to smile. Customers came and went, talking about the persistent fog and the lack of rain. The five-and-dime was closing, but a new pharmacy was taking over the space. Renee, a woman with eight children who came to the stand almost every day, carried over a plastic garbage bag full of hand-me-down clothes.

Mara squealed in delight. "Are there any dresses?" She opened the bag and started pawing through it.

"Thank you so much," Shoshanna said, taking the bag from Mara and putting it underneath the counter. "Mara and I will go through them later."

"I hope you can find some things you like in there," Renee said. "The kids grow like weeds. Some of those things still have tags on them. Let's see...I need two pounds of beans, Shoshie. And maybe a couple of artichokes. How're you doing, Judy?"

"Pretty good. How about yourself?"

"Good. Wayne took the boat out yesterday and caught a full hold of salmon. He sold them for over three bucks a pound in San Mateo. That's over two thousand dollars in profit, when all's said and done."

"That's great. Hey, I'd buy some salmon from him if he's got any left."

"He didn't go out today. He said he had to stitch up the nets down at the marina, but I talked to my friend Yolanda a little while ago and she saw him at the racetrack. He's a fool. He finally makes a little money and then he blows it all at Bay Meadows. If he goes fishing tomorrow, which he will if he's not hung over, I'll be sure to bring some fish if he gets lucky again."

Shoshanna handed her the bag of beans. Judy threw in

another handful and winked at Renee.

"Thanks, ladies. See you tomorrow. Remember to take those clothes home and try them on. They'll come in handy when school starts next month."

Shoshanna started to wipe down the scale with a towel, while Mara took the clothes bag from beneath the counter and started to rifle through it again. "Don't mess everything up with your grubby hands, Mara. They're all clean and folded. We can look at them later when we're home," Shoshanna said. The word "home" stung her throat and hung in the air.

"Shoshie's right. Maybe you should wait until we get home to go through them, baby girl." Judy told Mara.

Shoshanna felt tears gather in her eyes. It all seemed too much to bear. There was Judy calling Mara "baby girl." People she barely knew were giving her clothes and talking to her about starting school as if she belonged here, like this was really home and she was really a normal kid. Then, at the other end of it, Ella was pacing around, threatening to pull up stakes and leave simply because she was bored.

"Shoshie, what's wrong? Is your stomach still bothering you?"

Shoshanna looked down at the floor, then out across the street. Anything to avoid looking into Judy's face, because she knew she'd start sobbing. "No."

"What is it, then?" Judy put down the basket of artichokes and walked over to Shoshanna. She wrapped her arms around her, pulling her in. That was it; Shoshanna crumbled. She started to cry—huge, gut-wrenching, heaving sobs. "What's wrong, baby? Tell me."

"Ella doesn't want to stay here. She wants to take us back to San Francisco. She…she said farming's not her thing. She's *bored*."

"Oh, honey." Judy looked stricken. "Don't you worry. I can talk her out of that. She can't just take off by herself, and she can't make you go with her. Well, maybe she can, but she shouldn't. We all worked so hard to get settled here, and we're just getting started. Avery needs us. You guys can enroll at school. The Haight is nowhere for kids. I told her that."

"She doesn't care. I think she's got her mind made up that we're leaving."

"Shoshie, let me do the worrying. I can talk some sense into her tonight. She has to be able to see that living here is better for you and Mara. She has to see that you guys have a chance at a normal life here."

"She hates normal," Shoshanna said, wiping her nose with a piece of paper towel.

Judy nodded, smiling weakly. "Yeah, Shosh, I think you're right about that. But even if she hates it, I think

I can convince her that normal is the best thing for you two." A car pulled up to the stand. "A customer. Got to get a move on. Listen, just hang on. We'll get through this. You're not going anywhere, not yet."

Shoshanna sighed. She didn't know which was stronger, Judy's optimism or Ella's boredom-inspired restlessness, but she knew that at the end of the day, she would have to go with her mother and her sister. As much as she might want to think she had some control over her life, she knew that right now, both she and Mara were at the mercy of her mother's whims.

✳ ✳ ✳

Judy made macaroni and cheese for dinner. She added extra cream cheese and butter, and bread crumbs on top. Ordinarily, it was one of Shoshanna's favorite meals, but she barely managed to swallow a few bites. They talked about how busy the day had been out at the stand. For the first time ever, they had actually run out of artichokes. They had to wait a half hour while Avery loaded Fred and Dixon into the rear of the pickup and hightailed it to the field, where they picked artichokes like crazy.

"They were picking every artichoke they could get their hands on, ripe or not," Judy said, laughing. Then she told Ella about the bag of clothes Renee had brought.

"That's nice," Ella said. "They could always use some new stuff, and nothing beats free."

"How do you like my dress?" Mara said, standing up and showing off what she'd pulled from the bag, a pink paisley with puffed sleeves.

"Nice," Ella said. "You look like a princess."

"I know," Mara said. "And Shoshie's wearing one of Renee's shirts. There were lots of things we liked."

Judy started to clear the table. "Renee said they could wear them to school in September."

Ella was silent. Shoshanna held her breath. Leaning back, Ella coughed, reached into her overalls pocket, and pulled out a crumpled pack of cigarettes.

Judy scraped the leftovers into the garbage. "I think school sounds like a good idea. The girls have to branch out, Ella. Learn. Make friends."

Ella got up and walked over to the stove. She turned on the front burner, lit her cigarette, and inhaled deeply. "I can teach them myself."

"Yeah, but you *don't*," Shoshanna said harshly, but no louder than a whisper.

Judy gave Shosh a knowing glance. "I'm sorry to be so blunt, El, but that's bullshit. You hardly have the energy to look after yourself. I have busted my ass getting us going down here. I found us this place; I found us work. The girls pitch in. I'm sorry to say this, and I've tried to be patient, but you aren't pulling your weight and you've got to start. I don't know what's gotten into you. When you lived on Clayton Street, you were always doing things."

Ella looked unperturbed. "Once I get some supplies, I'll start making jewelry. I really can't get started on anything yet."

Judy pounded her hand on the table. The plates and glasses shook. "You can get started on the picking and the weeding. You could get started on working at the stand. You can spend time being a mother to your daughters. We have landed in a good place, and you're determined to screw it up."

Ella shrugged. "What can I tell you, man? Farming's not my thing."

Shoshanna couldn't hold back anymore. "Nobody cares about that, Ma. Being a good parent should be your thing. Moving from place to place to get away from my own shadow is not *my* thing. Moving around like nomads isn't my thing, and it should not be your thing or Mara's thing either." Shoshanna could feel her body shaking.

Judy placed a hand on Shoshanna's and spoke in a softened voice. "They're kids, El. They have to be able to set down roots. That's how kids grow, like flowers.

Community is important. That's why we loved the Haight when it was going strong. Remember the summer of 1966? We were all like family. Even though you knew Adam was bad news, even though you left under bad circumstances, the people you took with you were people you cared about. That's why you went to Sweet Earth Farm, not for Adam's messed-up reasons. You had faith. At least, that's what you told me back then. A group of people working the land together, remember? You were all going to take care of each other."

Ella traced her finger along the table's chipped surface. "Yeah. And look how that kind of faith panned out."

"But this is different. This can work. Just give Half Moon Bay and the farming life a year. That's all I'm asking. One year. And please, let the girls go to school."

"I'll give you till September. That's three months. And no school. I don't want any records that we exist, and that includes medical records or IDs or anything."

Judy stood up. Her face was flushed. "Why? Why? I don't get it."

Ella took a deep breath. "Okay. Number one, there is no Mara, as far as the U.S. government is concerned. She was born in my bed. No birth certificate or anything. I want to keep it that way. Why should I welcome Big Brother into her life if I don't have to? If I register her for school, they're going to want all that shit, and I'm telling you now, I won't comply."

"There's no me?" Mara looked to Shoshanna, terrified.

"Of course there is, Mara. It's okay. That's not what she meant." Shoshanna gave her sister a smile, which calmed Mara just enough.

"She's going to have to deal with documents at some point. How is she going to learn to drive or get a job or vote?"

"It's not hard to live outside the system. There are thousands of us dissidents. Lots of the Sweet Earth kids aren't documented. I'm not worried. Shoshie's got a birth certificate but she never got all those shots. Adam read a whole bunch of stuff that proved that vaccinations are unnecessary, unhealthy, and a government and drug company conspiracy."

Judy shook her head. "Like Adam ever told you the truth about anything? Jesus, Ella, think about this. You're just putting off the inevitable, and you're putting it off onto Shosh and Mara."

Ella shrugged. "You just don't get it, man. And speaking of Adam, that's another thing. I've got that whole evil trip breathing down my neck. I don't want to make it easier for him to track us down. He doesn't need me to provide a road map of official forms to find us. If there aren't any dots, there are no dots to connect. We need to stay invisible."

"Maybe we can make up names. What if we say we're someone else?" Shoshanna asked. "People get their names changed all the time. And anyway, Ma, I'm not a baby anymore. I don't want to live outside the system. I want to live with the kids who come to the stand, the kids I see every day, the kids in *Seventeen* magazine. Don't I get to choose my life? You're always talking about free will, and you won't let me or Mara have any."

"Dream on, Shosh. You don't understand the way things work. The system doesn't work for those who don't buy in. They hate us because we threaten them. They hate us because we aren't accountable to them. They hate us because we operate outside of them and their lame-ass rules." Ella looked at Shoshanna and touched her hand. "They're never going to accept you for you. You're always going to be an outsider.

"Baby, I'm sorry. Listen, I swear I'll get you books when we move to San Francisco. You can even look into going to the Free School. Mara too. But I can't risk having you go to school. Radar. You know what I'm talking about. Adam's got his ways. We feel safe here because Adam doesn't know where we are, and it's easy to forget about everything. Right? But you've got to remember."

"Come on, I know it was bad, but you can't go around being paranoid," Judy said. "I mean, Adam's a lowlife scumbag, but he's just a human being, not a demon."

"That's what you think," Ella said darkly.

Shoshanna knew too well what Ella was talking about. She saw Ella curled up in a pool of blood on the barn floor. She remembered waiting in the rain for hours by the back door when he wouldn't let her in the house because he was tripping or with some woman. The dog shot in the head, lying by her feet as she ate dinner, his trusting eyes staring up at her, then going blank, and Adam's only reason for pulling the trigger was he didn't like the way the dog smelled.

Then, just before they left Sweet Earth, the conversation she and Ella had walked in on. "She's only fourteen, but she's almost ripe," Adam was telling Reed, passing him the hash pipe. "Give her a month or two, then I'm cool with you being her first. She's yours for the taking. My gift." Ella's face had gone blank. She'd just walked to their room, and two days later, they'd made their escape. Shoshanna shook her head to try to erase the memories, but she could still hear Adam's voice, smooth as a long sip of cool water when he wanted something, sharp and cutting as jagged glass when he was angry.

"I want to stay here too," Mara said, reaching for

another piece of bread. "I think you could learn to love it, Ma. Maybe you need to play with Laddie more."

"September, Mara," Ella said. "You have till September. What do you say we change the subject? Grab some paper and pencils. Enough talk. Let's draw."

As Mara scurried off for the paper and pencils, Shoshanna felt something in her chest ease. Time might change Ella's mind. Three months was a start. Maybe between now and September, their fortunes would shift, and things would change.

CHAPTER EIGHT

July was more than half over. The artichoke and bean crop had done well, better than ever, Avery told them. "We didn't even need the sunshine, because you ladies brought your own." More people came to Avery's stand, initially because it looked inviting, and then they kept returning because they got to know Judy and Ella and the girls. There seemed to be a community consensus that the vegetables were the best around, and Avery's prices were fair.

Avery had tried something new this year. He'd cleared two acres for pumpkins. One of the neighboring farms had done that with spectacular results, and Judy convinced him to give it a try. The pumpkin patch was burgeoning, buds everywhere on the thick green vines, and everyone could tell that come autumn, barring a drought or earthquake or some other catastrophe, they would have a banner crop.

Judy kept a nervous eye on Ella, worried that she would try to take off with the girls before September. Judy had already started fretting at the prospect of leaving in September, because she wanted to help Avery with the pumpkin harvest. She knew how much Avery depended on them, and she couldn't bear to think what a blow it would be to him when they left.

Ella returned to the fields and the stand with enthusiasm, but she found she just didn't have any stamina. She would complain of being light-headed, and her appetite was off. She seemed to suffer from a chronic sore throat and dry cough, and everyone—Avery and the girls, and even the customers at the stand—lectured her about her smoking.

"Cancer sticks" was what Mary, a stand regular, liked to call cigarettes. That and "coffin nails." Avery supplied Ella with her weekly carton, while at the same time admonishing her. "Do as I say, not as I do," he said, "Quit. Here's a carton." Ella just laughed and thanked him for keeping her sane.

Shoshanna tried not to think about anything past September. It wasn't easy, because she was a worrier, but she found that trying to live in the moment gave her a measure of happiness she'd never had before. She kept thinking that if she did things happily and well, made no waves, just did her job and asked for nothing, Ella might not even notice that time was passing. She might relax enough that she'd end up forgetting all about her plan to leave. Shoshanna had once heard the expression "walking on eggshells," and that's what it felt like. But if it meant they might be able to stay, she'd keep treading lightly as long as it took.

Then Jim Benjamin showed up. It was a foggy Tuesday morning, much the same as the foggy Monday morning that preceded it. The time was just past ten, and customers hadn't started to drive up and drift in. Judy and the girls were working in the stand, sorting green beans into premium, mid-range, and damaged. It wasn't hard work but it required patience and concentration.

A car drove by and slowed down. "Someone's here," Mara announced. "Can I bag? I'm tired of looking at beans."

"Sure," Judy replied, looking up. She grinned. "Hey! It's Jim!"

Mara ran out and gave him a hug.

"Man. You ladies look like you're in your element," Jim told them.

"We love it here." Shoshanna smiled.

"Thanks for turning us onto it. It's cool—Avery's out-of-sight," Judy said.

"Yeah, I suppose he is cool, for an old guy," Jim said.

"He's cool, period," Shoshanna replied. "Did you

drive out for some beans? Artichokes? We haven't seen you in ages. How's Francine?"

Jim shrugged. "Good, good. She's back at the shop working. Hey, there's an actual reason I'm here. Is Ella around?" Jim opened a bag of beans and looked inside.

"Take a bag, Jim." Judy waved her hand above a row of beans on the stand. "On the house. The ones on the right are the best. Ella should be out any second."

Ella opened the screen door and walked over slowly. Over a long denim skirt, she wore a ratty maroon sweater of Avery's with suede elbow patches and a bright red knitted scarf. The sweater sagged down to her knees. In the morning light, Shoshanna noticed that her mother's eyes were ringed by purple-black circles. Her thin face looked bloodless, almost gray. Ella coughed and turned her head to spit onto the packed dirt of the driveway. Shoshanna turned away.

"Hey, Ella. Just the person I want to see."

"Hey, Jim." Ella smiled wanly. "It's been a while."

"Yeah. Hey, are you okay? You don't look well."

"I don't know what I've got. I just know I feel like crap."

"You should see a doctor about that."

"I don't do doctors. The body can heal itself."

Jim reached into his pocket. "I have something here that should make you feel better. Over a hundred dollars for your jewelry. Not bad, huh? Plus I have back orders for maybe a dozen more. If you're up for it, I can keep you busy for a while. Just try to get your hands on some sterling silver that wasn't jacked."

"Cool. I can do that." Ella fingered the bills and put them in her skirt pocket. "I figure I can hit the flea market on Sunday to get more silverware. Actually, Avery has a soldering iron that's better than my crappy torch. I should be able to get you a batch of bracelets and rings in no time." Shoshanna could see in Ella a faint glimmer of excitement that, in the moment at least, overcame the weariness. It was a start.

Actually, it turned out to be a good start. Over the next few weeks, it was as if Ella suddenly woke up and decided to make up for lost time. She seemed to regain her energy and started eating better. She cut back on her smoking, in large part because she was so busy with her hands, making jewelry.

One rainy Saturday, Shoshanna, Mara, and Judy helped her transform a small shed that had been used to store insect killer and leftover paint into a jewelry-making studio. Avery gave her a sturdy worktable that had been gathering dust in his basement, and she found a stool in the barn that had once been used for milking cows. One Saturday, they all went to flea markets, one in Half Moon

Bay and another bigger one in San Mateo. Ella bought up all the old silverware she could and, when she got back to the farm, set to work.

"Your mother must be feeling better," Judy announced as Shoshanna and Mara helped her pull weeds from around the wooden foundation of the stand. It was a sunny Tuesday afternoon, and the rush of customers had slowed to its usual midafternoon trickle.

"Yeah," Shoshanna said. "It's about time. I think she just needed some incentive."

"Yuck, look at the roots on this one," Judy said, pulling up a thick, stalky plant and jamming it in the weed bag. "Those belong on a *tree*, not a weed. Anyway, whatever it is, I'm just happy to see your mom excited about getting out of bed in the morning. She hasn't talked once about moving away from here, which is great—I can talk to her about enrolling you two in school and she might not bite my head off." Judy sighed. "The only thing is, she's got to see a doctor about that cough. Avery and I were talking about it. We don't like the sound of it."

"She won't see a doctor. She thinks conventional medicine is part of a government conspiracy."

"That makes no sense at all, you realize," Judy said. "Doctors don't work for the government."

"I agree with you, but try telling her that," Shoshanna

said. "She wouldn't even take the medicine they gave her when Adam got her sick."

"What medicine?"

Shoshanna shrugged. "I think it was called penna-something-or-other. It was for when she got really sick from something Adam gave her. It was when he was living in the main house and we had to stay in the little barn because for a little while he liked these two girls, Willow and Starr, better than he liked Ma."

"Willow and Starr?"

"They were two girls who hitchhiked up to Sweet Earth from someplace called Reno. They used to be waitresses at the Holiday Inn. That's what they told me. They didn't talk to us much other than that, but my mom hated them."

"Uh-huh." Mara nodded. "She tried to kill one of them with a pair of scissors. I think it was Starr. Was she the fat one with the curly hair, or the skinny one with the funny eye?"

"The fat one. They finally took off and Adam moved back in. And when he did, he and Ma were both sick. He had to take medicine for it and he gave her the same medicine, but she wouldn't take it. She threw it down the hole in the outhouse."

"Jesus," Judy said.

"Don't worry. It was okay. She got better. She was right. She didn't even need the medicine." Mara wiped a little ball of sweat off the tip of her freckled nose. "I'm tired of weed pulling, Judy. Don't you think this is good enough?"

"I guess so, Mare Bear. Go inside and wash up, okay?" Mara trotted off, looking relieved. "How 'bout you, Shosh? Ready to call it a day?"

"Sure. It looks better, doesn't it?"

"Yeah." Judy stood up and put her hands on her hips. She stretched out her back and yawned. "Man, honey, the more I find out about how you were living, the more relieved I am that you guys escaped from Sweet Earth. There's no telling what could've happened to you."

Could have? "Uh-huh."

Just then, they heard Mara's voice, shrill and frightened. She was leaning out of the barn door, jumping up and down.

"Shoshie! Judy! Something's wrong with Ma!" Dropping the weed bags, they ran over. Mara's face was pale and her chest was heaving with sobs. "She's in the kitchen. She's on the floor and she's asleep, and I can't wake her up."

Judy ran ahead into the kitchen. When Shoshanna got to the door, she saw Judy drop to her knees and place her hand gently on Ella's neck. "She's alive. She must have fainted or something. Girls, can you run over to Avery's and ask him to help you call an ambulance? I think your mother needs to get to a hospital." Shoshanna just stood there for a moment, looking at her mother's face, which was almost gray. "Go on now, Shosh. I'll stay with her. I think she needs to go to the hospital."

Shoshanna and Mara ran to Avery's house, throwing open the back door and running right into the kitchen, screaming his name. There was no answer. Shoshanna looked out the window at the driveway. "His truck's not here!"

"What do we do?" Mara asked, starting to cry.

Shoshanna ran to the telephone. Hands shaking, she dialed the zero.

"What are you doing?" Mara sobbed.

"I saw this on TV," Shoshanna said. "Zero gets you to the operator."

"Operator. How may I assist you?" the voice on the phone said.

"I need an ambulance for my mother. She's really sick."

"I'll connect you to emergency services."

After one ring, a woman answered. "Emergency services dispatcher. What is your street address?"

What was their address? Shoshanna had no idea. Panic welled in her chest. "I don't know! We're in Half Moon

Bay. Avery Elliot's farm. It's the one with the vegetable stand in front. It's got flowers painted on it."

"Now, honey, I'm sorry but I'm going to need for you to give me an actual street address. Do you see the number on the house or the mailbox? I can't send an ambulance over to a vegetable stand."

"Mara, run. Run as fast as you can and find the numbers on the mailbox for me. Remember them and come back so I can tell the ambulance where to go. Hurry!"

"Good job, honey," the operator said. "Now, what's your name?"

"Shoshanna."

"That's a pretty name. Shoshanna what?"

As always, Shoshanna felt a surge of panic when she was asked for her last name, but she knew this was an emergency, and she just said it.

"Okay, that's Ebersole with a *b* as in boy?"

"Yes." Where was Mara? This was taking her forever.

"Can you describe your mother's symptoms?"

"She fainted. She's breathing but she's not awake. I don't know what happened. We weren't home."

Just then, Mara screamed into the kitchen: "One, five, five, one. It's on the mailbox. One, five, five, one." Mara ran back into the kitchen, cheeks flushed and panting. "One, five, five, one. It's painted right up there on the mailbox!"

Breathlessly, Shoshanna repeated the number to the dispatcher. "One, five, five, one, Route One, the long dirt driveway off Route One. Elliot's Farm. Out back there's a big green barn and that's where we live. My mom's in there."

"You're sure she's breathing?"

"Yes."

"That's good. You were so smart to call. I'm sure she's going to be okay. Is there someone with her now?"

"Yes. Our friend Judy."

"You and your sister wait by the mailbox so the ambulance will see where to turn, okay? Bye, now, and I am hoping that everything will be okay for your mom." Shoshanna hung up the phone. "We have to stand out front, Mare, to wait for the ambulance."

"Is she going to be all right, Shoshie?"

"She'll be fine," Shoshanna said, trying to put any doubt about her mother's recovery out of her mind. "She just has a bad cold and she's weak. That's all."

"But she never didn't wake up like this before. Do you think she's gonna die?"

Shoshanna started to walk to the door. "No, Mara. Don't even say things like that. She just needs some medicine and to see a doctor. She'll go to the hospital, get a checkup, and then she can come home. Come on. We're supposed to wait by the mailbox."

They were waiting for less than ten minutes when they heard the ambulance siren making its way toward them. They motioned for it to turn in, then ran behind it back to the barn.

When they went inside, they saw Ella sitting upright and conscious. She was arguing with Judy, shaking her head from side to side. She started to cough, and Judy handed her a napkin. She spat into it, and Shoshanna watched as the napkin turned red.

"That does it, Ella. God damn. Look at that blood. Jesus Christ. When are you going to admit you're sick? What if you have pneumonia? You have to see a doctor."

"Don't die, Ma. Please, Ma." Mara started to cry hysterically. She ran to her mother and threw her arms around her neck. Ella just sat there, slumped over, too drained to return the hug.

"Mara, I'm not going to die. Judy is just being dramatic. Fine. I'll get myself checked out. I'll see a doctor, if that's what it takes to shut everyone up. I'll take an ambulance ride to the hospital and let them poke at me and run a bunch of useless and expensive tests until they figure out I have a cold and charge me, like, five thousand bucks and tell me to go home, quit smoking, and drink orange juice." She glared at Judy. "You're going to look pretty stupid. And you're going to owe me money."

"I hope I do look stupid. I would like nothing more than to look stupid. It would be my pleasure to owe you money."

Two men knocked on the screen door, carrying an oxygen tank and wheeling a gurney. They rushed in without waiting for an answer. One man was enormous and looked like he was having trouble breathing himself. The other was scrawny with a tense look on his face. The fat one spoke first. "Are you all right, ma'am? Our report says you were unconscious."

"Unconscious? Try sleeping. Yeah, I think my friend is just freaking out unnecessarily. I had the flu real bad last month, and I guess I didn't get over it yet."

"Just to set the record straight, she didn't have the flu, and she was unconscious when we found her and she's been coughing up blood," said Shoshanna.

"That's right," Judy said.

"Those are serious symptoms, ma'am. Your friends here are right to be concerned. Now, if you all wouldn't mind, you folks need to go into another room so's we can move in our equipment. Fred, you got the oxygen?" Fred nodded. "We're going to take you over to the hospital in Burlingame, okay?"

"Do I have a choice?" Ella tried to stand up, but fell back weakly into a heap on the floor. Putting their hands under her arms, the two men lifted her onto the gurney. She grimaced in pain. "Careful, my ribs are pretty sore." Shoshanna ran to hold the door open for them.

Suddenly, Ella gasped. "Wait. Wait. Seriously, just leave me here. I'm broke. I can't pay for this."

"I'll take care of it," Judy told the men. She bent down and touched Ella's arm. "Between Avery and me, you're set. Don't worry."

"Mom—" Shoshanna couldn't get any words out. She felt a sudden wave of panic wash over her, causing her stomach to knot up and her heart to race. She knew the hospital was the last place her mother would want to go, and she must be frightened that something really was wrong to agree to being brought in.

"Your mother is going to be fine, sweetie. We'll visit when Avery gets home 'cause we'll need to borrow his truck, and then you can see for yourselves what a good place the hospital is. Now give her a kiss, and we'll go back to the house and wait for Avery." Holding hands, they walked across the yard and watched Ella's departure through the kitchen window.

"Do you think they're going to turn the siren on?" asked Mara, as the ambulance started down the driveway. Flashing lights and a loud wail answered her question.

"This was scary but I think it's a good thing."

Shoshanna squeezed Mara's hand. "Right, Judy?"

Judy answered, "Yes. The doctors will check her out and be able to give her some medicine and she'll get a chance to rest. They might even convince her to quit smoking. I know she didn't want to go to the hospital, but it was the right thing to do."

Judy looked around the kitchen, trying to think of something to distract the girls. "Hey, do you guys want to make some fudge? We have the ingredients. Then we can bring your mom some when we go to visit. I know she's against chocolate, but it's impossible to resist fudge. Come on."

"Sure," Shoshanna said. Mara shrieked her approval. It seemed as good a way as any to pass the anxious time.

Judy was carefully placing the fudge—still warm with several fingerprint indentations, courtesy of Mara who insisted on tasting the finished product—into the refrigerator when they heard Avery's truck pull up. Both girls ran outside.

"Evening, ladies," Avery said as he slowly opened the door.

"Can you take us to the hospital?" blurted out Mara, hopping on one foot.

"Now, that's an unusual request. Why would you want to go there?" asked Avery.

"Our mom had to go in the ambulance because she's sick," Mara told him. "She was asleep on the floor and we couldn't wake her up, so we called and they took her away."

Avery leaned against the side of the truck. "Oh, man. Wow. I'm sorry to hear that. Of course we can go visit her."

"Thanks, Avery," Shoshanna said. "I know you must be tired. I'm sorry Mara just jumped on you like that."

Judy walked over. "We don't want to be a burden here. I mean, eat your supper. I'll even make you something. We made a batch of fudge while we were waiting for you. If you'd rather, you can just stay here. If you don't mind, I can borrow the truck and drive to the hospital. You don't have to come. You look tired."

"Yeah, I'm tired," Avery said. "I've had a tough day myself, to tell you the truth. But I'd do anything for you gals, you know that. I want to check on Ella too. Give me a minute to wash up."

The drive to the hospital took almost an hour. Avery was quiet, so Judy fiddled with the radio to fill the silence. Mara fell asleep. Shoshanna felt too uneasy to make conversation or doze, so she passed the time staring out the window. Avery cleared his throat. "Sometimes life is too hard," he said.

"Yeah," Judy agreed. She patted his shoulder. "You know our troubles. What's going on with you?"

Avery sighed. "My son, Dave, lost his job. He's down on his luck, and I'm afraid he's going to start drinking and drugging again. I thought things were going to be okay, but he called this morning and said he's out of cash and he's about to get evicted from his place in L.A. Says he wants to come back to the farm. I don't think he wants to come back. It's more like he has no place else to go."

Judy was quiet for a moment. "He used to live where we live, in the barn, right?" Avery nodded. "Will he want his place back? Maybe we could move out, find a cheap rental somewhere…"

"You're staying right where you are. You and Ella and the girls are family to me. Dave is coming back alone. The two-bit tramp he was shacking up with hit the road with some fella, so Dave can stay in the house with me. There's plenty of room. I just worry that he's never going to dig himself out of the hole he dug for himself."

"Hold on, here's the off-ramp for Burlingame," Judy said. "Yeah, I know what you mean. It just takes some people a little longer to figure out what they want, you know? I mean, look at me. After twenty-three years, you'd think I have some kind of clue about what the future holds. But I don't. It's a work in progress."

The hospital lobby was filled with potted palm trees. The linoleum floor smelled like disinfectant and floor wax. Under the harsh green-white fluorescent lighting, a heavy-set, bespectacled woman sat behind a desk. She smiled at the girls when they walked in. "I see some lucky patient is getting a nice visit," she said.

"That's right," Judy replied. "We're here to see Ella Ebersole." The receptionist nodded and looked down her list of patients.

"Hmm. There's no one here by that name. Are you sure you have the right hospital?"

"Try Ella White," said Shoshanna.

"Bingo," said the woman. "Room 303. Go down the hall, take a right, the elevators are on the right, go to the third floor. It's the room right across from the nurses' station."

On their way up in the elevator, Judy nudged Shoshanna. "Ella White?"

"Yeah. That's the name she uses when people ask her for her last name. I don't know why she chose it. She just made it up."

"It's because of Adam," Mara said quietly. "It's so he won't find her."

And it's the opposite of his heart, Shoshanna thought to herself.

The elevator came to a stop. "Here we are. Let's go visit your mother."

Shoshanna was not prepared for what she saw. Ella lay in bed, her eyes closed. She had two tubes leading into her arm. One was red, the other clear. Oxygen was flowing from a tank into her nostrils. Another tube snaked mysteriously under her blankets and seemed to be connected to a bag fill with a yellow fluid.

"Is that pee?" Mara asked, horrified.

"I think so," Judy said. "That's what they have to do when you're in the hospital, because you can't get out of bed to go to the bathroom. Don't worry. Your mom can't even feel it." Ella's eyes fluttered open. "Hey, there. If it isn't the elusive Ella White."

"You found me," Ella's voice sounded soft and raspy, like fingernails scraping against sandpaper.

"Don't talk. Relax. We just want to sit with you and send some love vibes your way. Avery's waiting downstairs, dozing, and visiting hours are only until eight, so we won't be here long. Avery wanted to come up to visit, but they only allowed three visitors, so he said to give you his regards and he'll stop by tomorrow."

Shoshanna stood next to her mother and tried to come up with some words of encouragement. She couldn't think of anything. Then a tall woman with cropped brown hair, wearing a doctor's coat and silver wire-rimmed glasses, peered in.

"Oh! Hello there. I'm Doctor Huang. Are you Mrs. White's family?"

"Yes," Judy said quickly. "I'm her sister, Judy"—the lie came easily, without hesitation—"and these are her daughters."

"Hello, girls. I'll be taking care of your mother. I'll leave you all to visit for a bit," she told Judy. "Ella is very tired, though. And before you leave, Judy, would you stop by the nurses' station so I can talk to you? I need to see you without the girls present."

"Sure." Judy nodded, reaching across the thin hospital blanket for Ella's hand. "Come on, Shoshie and Mare Bear. Give your mom's hand a squeeze. Careful of the tubes, though."

Shoshanna touched her mother's hand and held it gently. It felt cold. The corners of Ella's mouth twitched and tried to lift, but Ella was too weary to manage a smile. Mara's grubby hand joined Shoshanna's. "I love you, Ma," she said. "I'm going to bring you cigarettes next time."

"I don't think that's a good idea, Mare," Judy said. "Maybe this would be a great time for your mom to quit. Listen, girls, I hate to cut this visit short, but I think your mom needs to rest. I think we should get going and let her sleep. Ella, we'll be back tomorrow." Ella gave no sign of hearing anything. Her eyes had closed and she seemed to have drifted off again. Judy touched Ella's shoulder, bony and lax under the thin hospital blanket. The girls did the same. Shoshanna bent over and whispered into her mother's ear.

"I love you, Ma. See you tomorrow."

Back in the hallway, Judy took Shoshanna and Mara to the vending machine and let them choose whatever they wanted. Mara picked her favorite, a Three Musketeers bar, while Shoshanna chose some gum.

"Okay," Judy said. "I have to talk to the doctor. It won't take long. Do you two want to wait here, or do you want to go hang out downstairs with Avery?"

"We'll wait here," said Shoshanna. "I think we should let Avery sleep too."

It didn't take long. Less than five minutes later, Judy emerged from the nurses' station, her eyes red rimmed and puffy. "C'mon, girls. Let's get Avery."

"What did the doctor say?" Shoshanna asked.

"When can she come home?" Mara said, framing the question around a mouthful of chocolate.

Judy spoke slowly, like the words were an effort. "I don't know, girls. Your mom's very sick. Sicker than she thought. Shosh, I'm going to need to talk to you. Some grown-up stuff, Mare. We can do that later. Come on, though. We shouldn't keep Avery waiting." She turned away and started walking quickly down the hall. The girls had to run to keep up.

They were back on the highway when Avery suggested stopping at the Half Moon Diner for dinner. Judy thought they should get home. "My treat," Avery said. "I don't want you having to cook when you get home."

"Well, I'm hungry. I'm *starving*," whined Mara. Shoshanna was too, but she didn't say anything. She had a weird feeling in the pit of her stomach. Something felt unsettled and ominous. She didn't like the way Judy was acting. She didn't have a good feeling about whatever it was that Judy needed to talk to her about.

"It's up to you, Judy," Avery said. "I figure that the girls got to eat anyway."

"You're right. Fine. Thanks." From the backseat, Mara cheered.

"Thanks, Avery," Shoshanna said quietly. She wished she could shake her feeling of apprehension.

The Half Moon Bay Diner was small but homey. There were eight booths and a counter. The floor was a cheerful red-and-white-checked linoleum, and the red vinyl booths looked inviting. The girls slid in across from Avery and Judy, and looked over the menu. After ordering cheeseburgers and fries all around, they sat back. Shoshanna looked at Judy's face.

"Why were you crying at the hospital?" asked Mara.

Judy shook her head. "I wasn't crying," she said, but not at all convincingly.

"Then why are your eyes all red?" Mara asked.

Judy pretended she didn't hear Mara's question. "Avery, you were telling me about Dave, and you said something else was bothering you. What happened?"

Avery sighed. "I think we've got enough to worry about with Ella in the hospital. You don't want to hear about my problems."

Judy put her hand on his arm. "We care about you, Avery. In case you didn't notice, we're like family. Wait, no, we're not like family; we *are* family, and families get through the tough times together. It doesn't break them; it makes them stronger."

Avery's eyes filled up. For a moment, Shoshanna thought he might start crying. Instead, he reached for the salt shaker and held it in his hand, which they could all see was trembling. "Looks kinda like the sand in an hourglass. Anyhow, girls, this is one of those tough times that I think I have to go through all by my lonesome. I went to the doctor today. My Parkinson's is getting worse, but I kind of knew that.

"The doctor told me how the disease progresses, and he's pretty sure I won't be around in a couple of years, least not around in any way I'd want to be around. He told me I should sell the farm or turn it over to someone." He sighed. "I hate to say it, because he's my own flesh and blood, but Dave's good for nothing. I'd like to give it to you, Judy, but I don't think you could manage the place on your own. It's just too damn big. Maybe you and Ella—"

Judy shook her head. "That's not going to happen."

"Why not?" Shoshanna asked. "It might, Judy. My mom's been so happy the last month, making her jewelry. So happy she hasn't talked about moving in a while. Maybe now we can convince her that we need to stay to help Avery." Then it hit Shoshanna. She knew what Judy needed to tell her.

"Staying's not the problem." Judy looked at Shoshanna.

"I know," Shoshanna said quietly. "I figured it out."

"Figured what out?" asked Mara.

"I don't know how to put this, Mare, except to come right out and say what Shoshie knows. Your mother isn't going to get better."

The waitress came at precisely that moment to find out if they wanted dessert, and the silence just hung there in the air while they waited for her to clear some of the plates and offer to come back with the check.

"She's dying," Shoshanna said, her voice harsh, hollow.

"Yes." Judy looked down at the heap of uneaten

food on her plate. "There's no easy or soft way to say it, girls. Yes."

"What does she have?" Avery's shaky fingers gripped the stainless-steel edge of the linoleum table.

"Cancer. It's called metastatic, meaning it started somewhere else and wasn't treated in time, so it spread to her lungs. It's advanced. Inoperable. Dr. Huang said it's a matter of weeks, not months." Judy looked out the window into the night, eyes narrowed as if she was looking for answers in the stream of passing headlights. "All they can do is make her comfortable."

"Shit," Avery muttered. Shoshanna was shocked. Some adults swore all the time, but she had never heard Avery swear, even when he was upset. He pushed himself up from the table, grabbed his coat from the hook at the side of the booth, and walked outside. She could see the plume of smoke above his head as he stood in the parking lot next to his truck.

Shoshanna felt the pit she'd had in her stomach since they left the hospital deepen and expand as the weight of Judy's words sunk in. The congealing fried food on the plates that hadn't been cleared yet was making her nauseous. Not Mara, who was looking at Judy blandly, uncomprehendingly, while chewing on a french fry.

Mara was clearly too young to understand this, the

finality of death, what it would mean to lose her mother. Shoshanna would have to be strong for her. But right now, she felt that she wanted someone to take care of her. She was losing her mother, and she desperately needed a mother. She felt her chest grow tighter and tighter. She couldn't breathe.

Shoshanna burst into tears and ran outside. She found a bench and sank down, head in her hands, and let her sobs shake her to her core. Avery walked over and sat next to her, resting his hand on her shoulder. After a while, she stopped crying, her sobs turning into hiccups. Between them, she struggled to catch her breath.

"There, there, honey," Avery said, wrapping his arms around her. She buried her face in his flannel jacket, which smelled like cigarettes and reminded her of her mother, which made her start to cry all over again. "Don't you worry," Avery said. "I promise you that you'll get through this. And even though this is going to sound strange, right now the thing I am wishing for is that this will be the most terrible day in your long and wonderful life."

CHAPTER NINE

The next morning was cool and the air was heavy with mist. Shoshanna thought it seemed like the sky was on the verge of tears, maybe to keep her company. She slid out of bed quietly and pulled on her work jeans and an old sweater. She didn't want Mara to wake up. Her own thoughts felt like enough to deal with.

Judy was in the kitchen, sitting at the table. She was drinking coffee and writing in a small spiral notebook. "Shoshie. You're up. It's still early. I was going to let you sleep."

"I couldn't sleep." Shoshanna poked her head out the back door. "It looks like it's gonna rain."

"Or the sun's going to come out. I think the weather can't make up its mind." Judy shut the notebook. "I know all of this feels like too much to take in. I know you must be worried about how you're going to get through this, and you've got to be worried about Mara too. But I've watched you with her, and I see just how loving and strong you are. You can do this, Shoshie."

"Thanks," Shoshanna whispered. "I'm just scared."

"We're all scared," Judy said.

"Are we going to have to go back to Adam?" Shoshanna asked. "I mean, he is our father…"

"No. Not in a million years. He's not a fit parent. Plus, he's a fugitive. Don't worry about that."

"And we'd never have to go back to Sweet Earth?"

"No. Never. But you do have relatives who live in New York. Your mother's parents. You've never met them, but they might want you and Mara to go and live with them."

Shoshanna shook her head. "No way. Live with strangers? Why can't we just stay here with you and Avery?"

"It's more complicated than that if you have blood relatives who claim you. I mean, they would have legal custody of you because they're your closest relatives. Your mom might actually *want* you to go live with your grandparents. We have to ask her. The last time they saw her was before you were born. They didn't even know she was going to have a baby. They don't know about you or Mara or moving to Sweet Earth. But soon they will. I think you are going to want them in your life, Shosh."

"How come my mom never mentioned them?"

"They had a fight. Your grandparents didn't trust Adam. They wanted your mom to come home and she wouldn't."

Mara wandered in. "What are you two talking about?"

"Just some stuff, Mara. And about how much we love you." Shoshanna smiled. "Come on in. How about a bowl of cereal?"

"Sure."

Shoshanna looked at the sister she had helped raise for years and worried for the sadness she would one day feel. But all she could say in that moment was something to make Mara laugh. "Your breath stinks," she told Mara. "It smells like a fart." Shoshanna pinched her nose and stuck her tongue out at her little sister. Mara started to giggle.

There was a knock on the kitchen door and Shoshanna ran to open it, threatening to tickle Mara as she walked by. "Good morning, Avery."

"Good if you like fog. It's supposed to lift in a couple of hours."

"C'mon in," Judy said. "I'm getting Miss Mara here a bowl of cereal. Want some coffee? I made a fresh pot."

"That'd be nice. But the reason I'm here is I want you to meet someone. You remember I was telling you about my son, Dave? Well, he surprised me by turning up on my doorstep late last night. I was telling him how you changed the place so he'd hardly recognize it, and I wanted to show him around. And introduce him to you and the girls, of course." Dave entered hesitantly.

"Hey, Dave. I'm Judy. C'mon in. I'll get coffee." Judy smiled and buttoned the top button of her shirt at the same time. "These two lovely ladies are Shoshanna and Mara. Shosh, could you get Dave a chair? There's that green one in the bedroom."

Shoshanna went to get the chair. When she returned, Judy was pouring coffee and Mara was sitting on the floor eating Rice Krispies, having graciously given Dave her chair.

"Dave, that chair is kind of shaky. Maybe you should swap for the one Shoshie has, and Mara can sit on hers. It's sturdier."

Shoshanna looked at Dave and thought that Judy's chair-swap suggestion was a good one. Dave was a big man. In fact, it was hard to believe he was Avery's son. As lean and brown as Avery was, Dave was pudgy and pale. Clearly, he was not a farmer or even someone who spent time outdoors or did any sort of physical work. Dave's eyes were the same intense blue as his father's, and they shared the same ruddy, rounded face, though Dave's was not etched by age, weather, and worry.

"Um, thanks," he said. His voice was surprisingly soft and gentle. "Nice job making this place livable. It was a dump when I lived here."

"You didn't spend much time cleaning, as I recall," Avery said. "You and that no-good tart."

Dave sighed. "Let's not start, Dad. Her name is Maria, and yeah, that whole relationship was a mistake that I'm still paying for."

"So, Dave," Judy said brightly, changing the subject, "what do you do?"

"Nothing. Well, right now I'm unemployed. Up until last month I was working in a bookstore. Just a little hole-in-the-wall place near Cal Poly in San Luis Obispo. The store lost its lease and I was out of a job. Last night I stepped out to buy some groceries, and when I came back, all my stuff was out in the front yard and there was a padlock on the door, along with an eviction notice. I don't get it. I was only a month behind in my rent."

Judy shook her head. "Wow. That stinks. But hey, it'll be great to have you here to help with the late harvest in a few weeks. The pumpkins are going to be unbelievable. It was a trial crop, but man, did it take off! Do you take milk or sugar?"

"Both, if you've got them."

Shoshanna and Mara left the grown-ups to their conversation and went into the bedroom to watch television. Shoshanna's attention kept drifting from Mighty Mouse on the screen to her mother in the hospital. Everything felt surreal. Did she make up last night? But when, after a half hour, Judy called out to them—"Hey, girls. How about making a couple of get-well cards for your mother? Dave just offered to drive us down to see her"—Shoshanna knew it was all too real.

"Sure. What did you do with the crayons, Mare?" Shoshanna looked on the bookcase where she'd left them the day before.

"I don't know. I think they're in the bathroom," Mara replied. "I can get them."

"Thanks. Then we can make ma some get well cards," Shoshanna said.

"Didn't you hear Judy last night?" Mara said, her lower lip beginning to tremble. "She's not going to get well."

Shoshanna hugged Mara tightly. "I know, baby. But she still needs cheering up. She'll still love knowing that we care about her, that we're here for her."

They made cards, Shoshanna's full of flowers, Mara's a portrait of Laddie, and on both, Shoshanna wrote, *Feel better, Ma. Get Well Soon.*

After they finished the cards and cleaned up the breakfast dishes, they all squeezed into Dave's car, a bright red Dart Swinger with a peeling black vinyl roof. Avery sat up front, and Judy and the girls found themselves crammed between a stack of pots and pans and a pile of what seemed to be dirty laundry.

"Sorry about all the crap back there," Dave said.

"That's okay. We're used to crap," Mara said cheerfully.

"Mare, that's not polite," Shoshanna said.

"But it's honest," Avery said. "And remember—we all appreciate honesty."

The drive to Burlingame wasn't long, and Shoshanna had no intention of whining about it, but sitting in the backseat with a toaster oven and an electric frying pan digging into her ribs made her feel as if the ride was some kind of weird torture that would never end. They were almost at the hospital when Mara turned to her. A lone Rice Krispie clung to her chin. "Shosh?"

Shoshanna reached over and brushed the cereal off. "Yes, Mare?"

"This morning I was watching TV and there was a man on a church show saying that Jesus can cure anything if you believe. Maybe if we believe, she'll get better."

"I guess there's always hope, Mare. I think we have to hope. But I also have to be honest. It doesn't look good." She saw Mara's face begin to crumple, and she put her arms around her. "One thing I can promise you is that I will be here for you. Like always." She attempted a smile. "Maybe Ma will feel better today, Mare. That would be nice."

"Maybe our cards will make her feel better," Mara said, and Shoshanna nodded, tears filling her eyes.

✳ ✳ ✳

When they arrived, the hospital parking lot was almost full. "There's a space." Judy pointed.

"Can I fit?" Dave asked. "It's pretty narrow."

"Hang on." Judy got out of the car. "I'll guide you in. I think there's room."

As she stood on the sidewalk directing the car, Avery cleared his throat, leaned closer to Dave, and said, "Now there's a good woman." Dave didn't say anything, but Shoshanna knew he must agree.

The hospital smell of disinfectant and floor wax was almost overwhelming. After buying a copy of the newspaper, Dave walked toward the lobby to wait. "We shouldn't be too long," Judy called after him.

He shrugged. "Take your time. It's not like I have anything else to do."

Judy reached into her purse and pulled out a worn paperback. "Do you like Vonnegut?"

"I've only read *Slaughterhouse Five*." Judy threw the book and he caught it with one hand. He glanced at it. "I didn't know he wrote short stories."

"Yeah. Some of them are pretty good." She looked over at Avery, who had taken a seat in a lobby chair and immediately begun snoring.

"He doesn't sleep at night," Dave said.

"I know," Judy said. "I see his light on all the time. I worry about him."

"I'm hoping I can help out some," Dave said. "Anyway, thanks for the book. And really, take your time."

Ella was dozing when they walked into the room. She was positioned on her back with the IVs draped over her, her head propped up by pillows but leaning to the right. The thin skin of her eyelids had taken on a yellowish hue and seemed almost translucent; the movement of her eyes was visible beneath them. Mara walked over to the bed and reached out to touch her mother's hand. Ella didn't even stir.

"You're back, I see," said a quiet voice from the doorway.

"Dr. Huang," said Judy, "how is she doing?"

"She's resting comfortably now." Dr. Huang turned to the girls. "Judy, can I see you out in the hall? We have some lab results back that I'd like to discuss with you." Judy nodded, following her out.

Shoshanna and Mara stood at the foot of the bed and, for a few minutes, simply watched their mother sleep. "Should we wake her up?" Mara asked.

"I don't think she would wake up, even if we tried," Shoshanna said.

A nurse came into the room. She took Ella's blood pressure and checked the IV drip.

"Is my mom going to wake up soon?" Mara asked.

"We gave her some sleeping medicine so she could be more comfortable," the nurse said.

"Can we wake her up? We want to talk to her." Mara touched Ella's hand again.

"I don't think she's going to be up for a while. Maybe not for a few hours. Do you girls want to wait in the visiting room down the hall? There's a television. I think there may be some art supplies and a few games. I can even try to snag you some milk and graham crackers."

"Thanks. That sounds like a great idea," Judy said, coming back into the room and reaching for Mara's hand. "Let's wait down the hall for a while, Mara and Shosh, and see if your mom wakes up in a bit. It's nice that she's getting some good rest."

Out in the hallway, Dr. Huang looked at Judy. "Have you talked to the girls?"

"Yes."

Dr. Huang looked at Shoshanna. "Then you understand your mom is very sick."

"I know she has cancer," Shoshanna said.

"That's right," said Dr. Huang. "And you know that means she's not going to recover." Shoshanna nodded.

"Unless there's a miracle," Mara said. "Like the man said on TV this morning. We can pray."

Dr. Huang looked at Mara. "Hope is always a good thing to have. Maybe I can talk to you," she said, turning to look at Judy, "and Shoshanna in the hall? Mara, honey, you stay here with your mom, okay? We'll be right back."

Dr. Huang took Judy and Shoshanna into the hall and shut the door behind her. "Judy, thank you for being candid with me about your connection to Ella. I had you pegged as more of a friend than a sister, to tell you the truth. Anyway, we ran some tests last night that tell us the cancer has spread further than we first thought. I told Judy this just now, when you and your sister were with your mom, and she told me that she is keeping you girls informed, and that she's committed to being completely open with you. Your mother will not be with us much longer, I'm afraid, so our job is to do everything we can to keep her free from pain. But this is something I need to tell you too, Judy, as well as Shoshanna. Legally, we need to try to contact the girls' father, because since he and Ella are still married, custody would go to him."

"That's not possible," Judy said. "He's not…involved in their lives right now. He's a murder suspect, and actually at this point, a fugitive. No one knows where he is. Ella does have parents, and I can contact them."

"Excellent," Dr. Huang said. "I think they need to know what's going on with their daughter. And even though I understand the precariousness of the situation, I will have to check with social services about our obligation to contact her spouse."

"Please don't try to get in touch with my father," Shoshanna told Dr. Huang. "It would be a very bad thing for me and my sister."

Judy put her arms around the girls. "Dr. Huang, I'll try to reach Ella's folks. But for now, maybe it's best that we go to the waiting room. We can talk more there."

Dr. Huang followed them into the waiting room and watched while Judy handed Mara a stack of paper and some crayons and Shoshanna a book.

Dr. Huang asked. "How old are you, Shoshanna?"

"Almost fifteen."

"I know this is going to be tough on you. But you seem like a strong young woman. I know you'll be a great big sister."

"She is a great big sister," Judy said. "You have no idea how great."

Dr. Huang looked at Judy. "We have a great social worker, Liz Henderson. She'll be in contact with you. Shoshanna and Mara will both need support. Actually, Judy, come out with me. I have some numbers to give you. The girls will be fine here for a few minutes."

"What are you doing, Shosh?" asked Mara.

"I'm reading, Mare. Do you want me to read to you?

"No. I want you to come down here and color with me."

Shoshanna sighed and put the book down. Maybe they would let her borrow it. It seemed like a good story, *Little House on the Prairie*, about a pioneer girl going West with her family. It would be nice to lose herself in a story, but Mara needed her. Shoshanna walked over and sat next to her sister.

"Look, Shosh, I drew this. It's you. See? It's you and Ma and me, when we used to pick apples. Remember all our plans?"

"I remember them, Mare. All of them." Taking a piece of paper from the stack, she began to draw a fairy-tale castle. She drew trees and a princess with long, dark hair. She drew a yellow sun and a blue sky. She drew the California her mother had painted in her mind—the orange trees, the flowers, the bright blue ocean—when they lived at Sweet Earth Farm. All that planning had led them not to paradise, but to this hospital, to this bittersweet moment. Ella saved her daughters but not herself.

Time passed, and the door to the waiting room opened again. Dr. Huang and Judy walked in. "What beautiful pictures," Dr. Huang said. "You girls are impressive artists."

"I know," said Mara.

"Thank you," said Shoshanna. One thing she was going to do, she thought, was teach Mara how to take a compliment. There would be time for that. "Wow, Mare, that's a nice horse."

"Cat," Mara said. "See the tail? But thanks."

"Girls, do you know where your dad is?" asked Dr. Huang. "The social worker told me I need to try to contact him about your mom's condition."

"Please don't get in touch with him," Shoshanna said.

"Why?" Dr Huang asked.

Shoshanna looked at her. "Because we're afraid of him."

"I'm not talking about custody anymore, Shoshanna. He would want to know your mom is sick."

"He wouldn't care," said Shoshanna. "I don't mean to sound rude, but you don't know him. You don't know Adam, what he's capable of. You've checked my mom, so you've seen she's had broken ribs and a broken nose. Look at the scars on her wrists. Can you understand why we can't let him know where we are? It isn't safe."

"One time he shot our dog," Mara said. "He shot him just because he smelled bad. He shot him right in the head in front of us. Then he made my mom clean it up. We really liked that dog too."

"That's what I was trying to tell you," Judy told Dr. Huang. "These girls have been through enough."

"Where is Ella's family?"

"New York City," Judy said. "Brooklyn, I think. Her name was Green. She told me she stopped talking to her parents over fifteen years ago, before Shoshanna was born. They had some run-in with Adam. Something about a stolen credit card and Ella's broken nose and black eye. They wanted her to leave him. She wouldn't."

Dr. Huang nodded. "Fine. You've convinced me not to contact Ella's husband, but we need to find her parents. I'm going to let the morphine wear off. When she's lucid, maybe she can tell us how to reach them." Dr. Huang stood up. "I have to make my rounds. You girls can go into your mom's room, but she seems to be sleepy today and I wouldn't wake her up. She needs her rest and it's better for her to be comfortable. We can call you tomorrow and tell you a good time to come, when she'll be awake. Judy, I have the phone number you gave me at Mr. Elliot's home. I'll be in touch."

When they went back to the lobby, Avery was still asleep and Dave was well into Vonnegut. "Back so soon?" he said. "You were right. These stories are good."

"Glad you like them," Judy said. "Vonnegut is far out. Thanks for driving us here, Dave. And thanks for being patient."

"No problem. Like I said before, the book is good,

and it's not like I have somewhere else to be."

Climbing back into the car, Mara stubbed her toe on the base of the metal fan and started crying.

"Are you okay?" asked Shoshanna and Judy in complete unison, and both put their arms around Mara at the same time. Judy looked at Shoshanna and smiled. In that moment, Shoshanna knew things were still not going to be easy but maybe, just maybe, they would be all right.

CHAPTER TEN

The next two weeks passed in a flurry of hospital visits and car rides between Half Moon Bay and Burlingame, interspersed with working the fields or manning the vegetable stand. By word of mouth, the regular customers knew Ella's prognosis and were especially kind to Shoshanna and Mara, telling them to keep the change and even giving them stuffed animals and other small gifts. The girls appreciated the presents, but even more, they appreciated being kept busy. The squash and zucchini crops were at their peaks, and Dave and Judy spent hours in the field picking them, often accompanied by Shoshanna, Mara, and Avery.

"Look, Shoshie, this zucchini looks like a mom that's having a baby," Mara said, holding it up.

"When they get too big like that, no one wants to buy them," Avery said. "Not as tasty. Too many seeds."

"I can make something with it," Judy said. "Zucchini bread or a casserole. I'll take it."

"Zucchini bread," Dave said. "Nothing personal, Judy, but somehow, my mouth isn't watering."

"Spoken like someone who's obviously never had zucchini bread. You don't know what you're missing. Why don't you and your dad come over for an early dinner? We can eat and then visit Ella afterward. I'll whip up a batch of zucchini bread and you'll see what you've been missing."

Shoshanna and Mara waited for Dave's response. They had grown to like having him around. He made them laugh. Even Avery seemed to be happier. Shoshanna watched a thin trickle of sweat run down Dave's face, through the stubble on his check, and down his neck beneath the collar of his T-shirt. His pale skin had tanned to golden brown in the sun, and he had gotten leaner from the physical work he was doing in the fields. He seemed to almost be enjoying the rigors of farm life, though he still complained about having to wake up so early.

He looked at Judy and grinned. "Sure. That'd be nice. Here, let me take the other side of the wheelbarrow for you."

"Thanks." They walked off toward the vegetable stand. Judy must have said something funny because they both started laughing, Dave so hard that he almost dropped the wheelbarrow.

"Do you think she likes him?" Mara asked.

"Uh-huh," said Shoshanna. "I think he likes her too."

"Maybe they'll get married," Mara said. "Really married. Not like Ma and Adam. Married for true love, like on TV."

"Maybe." Shoshanna picked up the zucchini basket. "We should go over to the stand. It's almost time for the after-work crowd."

The line of customers at the stand was unusually long because the squash and zucchini were popular items. Avery was there, hands shaky but weighing people's orders while Judy ran the cash register. When Shoshanna and Mara appeared, they were greeted with hellos. Dave helped people take the bags of vegetables back to their cars.

"How long are you sticking around here, Dave?" Shoshanna heard someone ask.

"Kinda depends," Dave said. "I was thinking about going down to L.A., but I'm in no rush. I kind of want to help see the pumpkin harvest through."

It was an hour before the crowd began to thin out. Judy left to start the zucchini bread, and Avery went inside for his late-afternoon siesta. Dave stayed out with the girls until the last customer left. Together, they shuttered up the stand and took in the cash box, which Dave let Mara carry back to Avery's house, a task that never failed to make her feel very important.

"I think today was a good day," she said. "This box has so much money I can hardly carry it."

"This was a record year for squash," said Dave. "Or so my dad says."

"I'm glad you're coming over for dinner," Shoshanna said. "So is Mara. So is Judy."

"So am I," Dave said. "I have to admit I'm still a little skeptical about the zucchini bread, but I guess we'll see."

"Judy made a chocolate cake with zucchini in it last night, and it was really good," Mara told him. "She even put chocolate chips in it."

Dave laughed. "Chocolate added to just about anything is an improvement," he said. "But give me a chocolate chip cookie any day. I don't see why you'd want to run the risk of spoiling perfectly good chocolate by throwing in a vegetable." He took the cash box from Mara. "Thanks, Mara. Man, you're right. It weighs a ton. I'm going to check in with my dad and we'll see you guys for dinner."

When the girls got back to the barn, the kitchen smelled like rosemary-and-sage-roasted chicken and potatoes and baking bread. Judy was running between the sink and the stove, her cheeks flushed, blond ringlets escaping from the confines of her braid in small wisps that clung to her face.

"It smells really good, Judy. Dave is going to love it," said Shoshanna.

"Thanks, Shosh, for saying so," Judy said.

"Do you like him?" Mara asked.

"That's a personal question, Mara," Shoshanna said. "It's not polite to ask."

"I don't mind, Shosh." Judy took the zucchini bread out of the oven. "Wow. This came out pretty perfectly, if I do say so myself. Yeah, Mare, actually, I do like him. I'm just not sure how I like him—as a really good friend or possibly something more."

Shoshanna smiled. "I think he likes you too. He looked really happy when you invited him over for dinner."

There was a knock at the door. "Speaking of which..." Judy said. "Come on in, guys."

The door opened, and Dave came in. "Guy, actually. Hi, everyone. I'm here solo for the time being. My dad's still resting. He was really tired from all the selling frenzy at the stand. He told me he's going to come over in a bit, when he feels ready to take on zucchini bread." Dave had changed into a new pair of jeans and a clean T-shirt. His hair was wet and he smelled like soap.

"Hey, Dave." Judy grinned at him. "You look sharp. I hope your dad makes it over soon, because once you've had a bite of zucchini bread—See it over there, fresh and warm from the oven? That's right, don't be shy, take a whiff. You know you want to—there won't be any left for him to sample."

Dave walked over to the bread, leaned down, and inhaled. "Damned if that doesn't smell incredible. I may have to eat a slice of humble pie along with it."

"We didn't make any humble pie," said Mara.

"Dave means he's going to owe me a big, heartfelt apology." Judy laughed. "Hey, girls, would you mind setting the table for five? I'm going to show Dave some of my hand-painted cards."

The girls set the table while Judy took Dave out to Ella's jewelry-making shed, where she kept her boxes of samples. Mara folded the pieces of paper towel that doubled for napkins while Shoshanna sifted through the drawer for the most closely matching forks and knives. They only had four plates, so she gave herself a bowl. "I'm starving," she announced. "I'm so starving I could eat an elephant."

"Sorry, we're fresh out of elephant. You'll have to settle for chicken," Judy said, opening the back door. "Dave, would you mind putting the salad out? The chicken and the zucchini bread are done, and I'll get the potatoes."

"Sure," Dave said. "I'm eagerly anticipating all this home cooking. So is my father. Maria—my old girlfriend, or as my dad likes to call her, 'that two-bit floozy'—hated to cook. Her idea of a home-cooked meal was heating up a TV dinner. Needless to say, we ate out a lot."

"That's convenient, but not very healthy," Judy said. "Eating out is expensive, and there are a lot of preservatives and other crap in frozen dinners. Sorry. I don't mean to get all preachy on you."

"Yeah, well, there was a lot of other unhealthy stuff going on back then. Preservatives were probably the least of my worries."

"Shosh, move the chicken to make room for the potatoes. Man, this looks good, if I do say so myself. We have to be sure to bring some of this to your mom, girls, even though her appetite's been off."

They sat across from each other, Shoshanna next to Mara, Dave next to Judy.

"This chicken is delicious," said Dave.

"Old family recipe," said Judy. "I've taken a vow of silence to never reveal it, but I'll let you in on the secret ingredients: mayonnaise and potato chips."

Avery came in. He still looked tired, but when he saw them all assembled around the table, he grinned. "What a great-lookin' group of folks," he said.

"Why, thanks, Avery. Sit down there at the head of the table. Can I get you something to drink? Water? Orange juice?"

"Water would be good. Thanks. So, where is this zucchini bread I've been hearing so much about?"

"Here," Shoshanna said and passed it to Avery. "Seniority. You get the first piece."

"It's got chocolate chips in it," Mara said. "My mom used to never give us chocolate. She always gave us carob. Judy loves chocolate."

"Yes, it's a terrible thing. I've corrupted you two. But carob's no substitute for chocolate. I'm sorry."

Avery took a bite. "I don't know if this will replace the fudge cake they serve at the diner. But it's pretty darn good. Try some, Dave."

"I will. I was waiting for you to test the waters." Dave took a bite and looked at Judy. "Mmmm," he said. "I'm not gonna lie. This is really good, Jude. You can hardly taste the zucchini."

Jude? Shoshanna thought. *Since when did Dave start calling Judy "Jude"?* And they seemed to be sitting very close together at the table. She decided a little salesmanship couldn't hurt the situation. "Judy's a really good baker."

"Thanks, Shosh. I don't know how good I am, but I'm adventurous. I kind of make up my own recipes. I mean, I made this particular recipe up. It may be weird to think of vegetables in bread, but—"

"What would you think of making a few batches of this bread and seeing if it sells at the stand?" Avery asked. "We have a lot of those zucchinis that aren't pretty enough to sell. That way they wouldn't go to waste."

"That's a great idea, Dad," Dave said. "Judy, if you made up a dozen zucchini breads, we can see if they'll fly."

"Sure," Judy said. "I'll need some ingredients."

"You can go shopping with Dave tonight, on your way home from visiting Ella," Avery said, reaching for the salad. "I was thinking of going to see her too, but if you could, just give her my regards and tell her I'll stop by with you all tomorrow. Tell her I'm sorry, but the old man is beat."

"I'll let her know, Avery, and I'll stop at the store. I can bake the zucchini bread first thing in the morning."

After dinner, everyone pitched in to help clean up. Shoshanna noticed Dave clearing dishes and washing them while Judy dried. That was something neither her father nor any of the men at Sweet Earth ever did. Even Avery, as weary as he was, wiped down the table and gave Shoshanna and Mara a kiss on the top of their heads before going back home. "Sorry to be a party pooper. Thanks for a wonderful dinner," he told Judy. Then he looked at her very seriously and touched her shoulder. "Thanks for everything."

✳ ✳ ✳

The drive to the hospital had become such a habit that Shoshanna felt the car could drive itself. Dave drove and Judy sat next to him in the front seat, while Mara and Shoshanna sat in the back. Shoshanna felt her body lean into and away from anticipated turns because she knew the route so well. In a way, as horribly painful and sad as everything was, there was a measure of comfort in knowing her mother was in a safe place, cared for by people who knew what they were doing, and free from pain and worry. She wouldn't let her mind to go the next step, the inevitable, but allowed herself to stay cocooned in a limbo of sorts.

"What do you think Adam would do if he knew Mom was sick?" Mara asked. The question surprised Shoshanna. She hadn't thought about Adam since talking about him with Dr. Huang.

"I don't know," Shoshanna said quickly, trying to banish any further speculation as quickly as she possibly could. But the thought returned and refused to leave. What if he found out somehow? Would that mean that when Ella died, he would come and get them and force them to go back to Sweet Earth Farm? Would he, as their father, have that right? What about their plan to start school in Half Moon Bay in a couple of weeks?

"Do you think he really does have radar like Mom says?" Mara asked. "Do you think he somehow knows where we are?"

"If Adam came here, I would call the police," Shoshanna said. "Don't you worry about that. Besides, no one we've met knows him or talks to him. If he hasn't found us by now, I don't think he ever will."

"Never mind Adam. How would you girls like some ice cream before we get to the hospital?" Dave asked. "Judy thinks maybe your mom would like a milkshake to go with the chicken and potatoes. What do you say we stop at Dairy Queen?"

They pulled in and Dave bought Mara what she requested: a vanilla cone with sprinkles. He also bought Ella a large strawberry milkshake. Judy and Shoshanna stayed in the car. "Are you sure you don't want anything?" asked Judy gently.

"No," said Shoshanna. "I ate a lot at dinner. I'm not hungry."

"You're so quiet, Shosh. Are you okay?"

"It's just that sometimes I almost forget about Adam. Up until Mara asked about him, I hadn't thought about him at all. It's like…up until my mom got sick, I was so happy here. I felt so safe. My biggest worry was that we couldn't stay. Now…well, I still feel safe most of the time because I make an effort not to remember certain things. It's like keeping them in a dark room and shutting the door. And when Mara said his name—"

"She's just worried about the future, Shosh. It's natural."

"I know, and I'm not blaming her. Really. I'm worried about the future too. It just makes it harder when I think about the past. It makes me always feel afraid, like I'm being stalked by a predator."

Judy turned around and leaned over the backseat, wrapping Shoshanna in her arms. She smelled like baking bread and fried potatoes and musk and patchouli, and Shoshanna thought she caught a whiff of Dave's soap. Judy buried her face in Shoshanna's hair and whispered fiercely, "Nothing's going to happen to you, Shoshie. Nothing. I won't let anything happen to you or to Mara. You're my family."

Shoshie started to cry because she felt the same way, and also because she knew that this new family in the process of being born had risen from the ashes of her old family.

CHAPTER ELEVEN

The hospital felt different that night—colder, more clinical. The smells were the same—disinfectant and floor wax. The fluorescent lights still hummed, but the glow they cast seemed even more bereft of warmth. The floor had been freshly waxed and buffed, and its surface looked as dangerous as ice. Even the woman behind the desk seemed distant. Usually she greeted the girls with a smile, but tonight she was on the phone, so she nodded distractedly and motioned them up to Ella's room.

Ella was awake and agitated. "What took you so long to get here?" she asked. Shoshanna was surprised that she seemed restless; usually when they visited at night, they had to rouse her from a sound sleep.

Mara and Shoshanna hugged her gingerly, avoiding the IV lines and the oxygen that clipped under her nose. Mara held her head and neck, and Shoshanna wrapped her arms around her mother's frail hips and rested her head on her stomach. Judy reached for Ella's hand. "Sorry we're late, babe. It was a crazy day at the stand. The zucchini and squash are like an avalanche. We stopped to get you a milkshake. Want a sip?"

Ella shook her head. "I have something to tell you," she said. They could see the panic in her face. "It's important. Adam was here."

"God, Ella! Are you sure?" Ella nodded. "How did he find you?" Judy asked. Mara started to cry. Shoshanna could feel her heart begin to pound.

"I don't know. He always does. He has his ways."

Adam has radar, Shoshanna thought. *It's true. My nightmare has come true.*

"What happened?" Judy asked. "What did he say? Where is he now?"

"I was sleeping and I woke up and he was standing over my bed like it was a completely normal thing that he was here. He was really calm. He said, 'It took me a while, but I knew I'd find you eventually. Have you heard the saying that "you can run but you can't hide"?'"

"What did you do?"

"I told him that I was really sick. That I'm dying. He just smiled."

"Sick bastard," Judy said.

"I told him that I need him to promise to leave you and the girls alone. But my voice sounded so weak." Ella looked fretful. "I wanted to yell at him, but everything I said sounded like a whisper. I don't think he even heard me."

"Is he going to come back?" Shoshanna asked, her heart pounding. "I'll call the cops, Ma. He's a wanted man. I can have him arrested."

"You didn't tell him where the girls are, did you?" Judy asked. "He doesn't know they're at Avery's?"

"No. I shut my eyes for a second and he was gone. I asked the nurse which way he went, and she hadn't even seen him because he slipped in and out so quietly, like a ghost."

"Don't worry, Ella," Dave said. "I'll find out where he is and talk some sense into him."

Shoshanna thought about the dog with the gun to his head. His sweet brown eyes. "Please don't, Dave. Adam's crazy."

"Well, I'm going to talk to the receptionist. She should never have let him up. Ella's only supposed to have visits from family." Dave turned and walked out. They could hear his sneakers squeaking down the length of the polished hallway.

"Girls, whatever happens, don't let Adam take you

back to Sweet Earth. Judy, don't let him take them. Kill him if you have to."

"Don't worry, El. The girls will never see Sweet Earth Farm again. They'll never see Adam if I can help it. I swear. And yes, I would kill him."

Suddenly the tension went out of Ella's shoulders. She wrapped a strand of Mara's hair around her fingers and patted the top of Shoshanna's head. "Thanks. You've never let me down, Judy."

"And I never will. Trust me on that, Ella."

Ella shut her eyes and seemed suddenly drowsy. "Tell me a story," she said.

"Remember when you used to tell us stories, Mama?" asked Mara. "Like the one about the magic castle in California. How there's always sunshine and candy to eat. Remember? And then we came here, and it's different."

Ella nodded. "Sure, baby. Once upon a time there were two beautiful princesses, Shoshanna and Mara..." And her eyes closed again. Her breathing seemed shallow and rapid.

"I'll tell you a story, El," said Judy. "Once upon a time there were two beautiful princesses, Shoshanna and Mara, one light, one dark, both beautiful. They were prisoners of the evil king. But one day, their brave mother, the noble Queen Ella the Lionhearted, rescued them despite great danger and took them on a long journey. There were surprises along the way, some good, some bad. Mostly good."

Shoshanna looked at her mother. All of the tension seemed to drain out of her face. There was a huge lump in Shoshanna's throat, but she refused to let herself cry.

Judy continued. "Luckily for the princesses, Queen Ella managed to lead them to a place where they would be safe from the evil king forever and ever, a place where she knew deep in her heart they would be loved and cared for. Love surrounded all of them. Love of family and friends and community and nature. Queen Ella sacrificed everything to bring the princesses to their new kingdom, and they were eternally grateful. Queen Ella kept on her noble journey and over time became an angel, a candle in a dark world that would burn in their hearts and spirits forever."

Ella's eyes were closed, and her breathing shifted from shallow and rapid to deep and steady. Judy whispered something in Ella's ear. Dave came back in and put his arm around Judy.

"Hallucination," he whispered. "They told me it's common with morphine. Nothing more. He was never here." Judy nodded. "Girls, I think we should let your mom get some rest."

"I love you, Mama," said Mara.

"Me too," said Shoshanna. "I love you so much." She leaned close and whispered into her ear, her voice cracking, "Thank you, Mama."

"It's time for her meds now," said a nurse. "She looks relaxed. Hopefully she'll get a good night's sleep. She was really upset about something today."

The call came at three in the morning. Avery answered it and woke Dave. Dave got dressed and walked across the yard to Judy's room. Together, when the sun came up, they told the girls.

CHAPTER TWELVE

The funeral was horribly hard for Shoshanna, but even harder for Mara. Somehow, even though Mara said she understood that her mother was dying, her death came as a terrible shock. She sobbed—huge, chest-heaving sobs—for hours, then slept with her arms wrapped around Shoshanna's neck in a stranglehold, as if afraid that in the night her sister also might suddenly vanish. Shoshanna didn't mind. Truthfully, she welcomed the ferocity of her sister's embrace. It felt like proof that they were still here and they had each other.

Judy took the girls out for dresses to wear to the funeral. Avery bought a plot in the cemetery down the road, across from the ocean, where his wife was buried, and arranged for his minister to come. Shoshanna liked that her mother would be laid to rest in a shady corner between a stone wall and a gnarled cypress tree. It felt like a protected spot, something Ella herself would seek out. The headstone was simple: Ella Green, June 15, 1940– August 3, 1972. Mother, Friend.

The stand's customers all came to show their love and support; there were close to a hundred people gathered together. Shoshanna, who had cried so much before the service and who would cry later when she was alone, on this day stood dry-eyed while Mara wailed, face pressed against Judy's hip. Judy stroked her hair. Dave put one arm around Shoshanna and the other arm around Mara.

When the minister said that Ella was free at last, Shoshanna wondered if perhaps he knew about Adam. She looked along the edge of the cemetery, at the cars driving past, and wondered if she would spend the rest of her life worrying that Adam lurked somewhere, waiting to take them back to Sweet Earth Farm.

Judy and Dave tried their hand at romance. For a few weeks, Dave was in the kitchen every morning, cooking breakfast, reading the newspaper, telling the girls to brush their teeth. His presence felt not like an intrusion but like part of the natural order of things. But when it came time for school to start two weeks later, Dave got a call from Maria, who had second thoughts about cutting him loose. She was in Los Angeles and wanted him to come back to join her. Dave was conflicted, horribly ambivalent, but even Judy had to admit that the farming life, which was in his blood, was not in his nature. He would never be comfortable taking over the farm. He had grown to love Judy, but Judy could tell that despite the tempestuousness of their relationship, he still loved Maria.

He packed up the red Dart one sunny Saturday morning in early September. Avery told Dave that he wished it had worked out, but he understood. He wanted nothing more than for Dave to be happy, and if this was what it took, he wished him well. Avery also mentioned that he had a backup plan.

Dave hugged the girls and promised to return. He pulled Judy aside. They both cried. In the end, it was Judy who told him to go, get in his car, and get back to his other life.

"Are you gonna miss Dave?" Mara asked.

"Yes. He was a good friend," Judy told her. "I'm not going to lie. It was nice to have him here. But I understand why he's leaving. And you know what? I have a feeling he might be back."

Shoshanna couldn't explain it, but she did too. She told Judy, and Judy smiled. "That's what they call a woman's intuition," she said. "Looks like we both have it."

Then Judy set about trying to enroll the girls in school. She knew it wasn't going to be easy. Not only was there no record of them, but she didn't want to contact anyone in Oregon who might set Adam on their trail. As she put it, she didn't want to open that can of worms.

"What does that mean?" Mara asked.

"I don't want your father to know you're here," Judy told her.

Shoshanna thought the image of Adam as a can of worms was pretty perfect. Still, she really wanted to go to school. The kids who came to the stand over the summer told her what happened in school—the things you could learn, sports you could play, even dances—and she couldn't wait to start. But to balance that against alerting Adam to their presence...that's when things got complicated. Did she want to be safe or live a life? She wished she didn't feel like she had to choose between the two.

A few days before school was to start, Judy told Shoshanna she had something to do at town hall.

Before she drove off in Avery's truck, she called out, "Hey, Shosh, it looks to me like you didn't quite finish making your bed. And when you're done, could you return the vacuum cleaner to Avery and maybe vacuum his living-room carpet while you're at it?"

"Sure." Shoshanna pulled the faded comforter over the sheets and grabbed the vacuum cleaner. Walking across the lawn, she noticed the clothes drying on the line—

Judy's flowered nightgown, her jeans, Mara's sundress. She thought for a moment about how the only things missing were Ella's work shirts and overalls.

Avery was sitting at the table, his reading glasses resting on the end of his nose, tracing the words on the newspaper with an unsteady forefinger. "Shoshie! What brings you here?"

"I'm returning your vacuum, but only after I vacuum the living-room carpet." Shoshanna plugged in the machine and went over the thin rug thoroughly.

"Perfect. Thank you so much."

"What's happening in the world, Avery?" Shoshanna asked.

"Nothing good. The war in Vietnam is a nightmare. Nixon's an idiot. No one can win it, and all those boys dying! The town wants to raise property taxes."

"Bummer. That's what my mother used to say," Shoshanna said.

Avery nodded. "There's a saying that the only things in life you can count on are death and taxes. The older I get, the more true that seems."

Shoshanna put her hand on his arm. "Unless you need me to get you anything, I'm going to get the stand ready to open. The pumpkins look really good. We picked a whole bunch yesterday. There's one that Judy thinks weighs forty or fifty pounds! I'm not sure where Judy went. She was all dressed up."

"Yep. I think she's trying to find out how to register you girls in school since you don't have birth certificates. She's been trying to call your grandparents in New York—"

Shoshanna looked at Avery with alarm. "But I thought it was all set and we were staying here—"

"Shoshie, I shouldn't have said anything. I didn't mean to worry you. Of course you're not going to New York. Judy wants you to live with her. It's just that when you have blood relatives who are still living, there are laws—"

"Well, I won't go live with people I never met thousands of miles away. Judy knows that. I'd take Mara and run away first." Shoshanna was shaking. She had been feeling so secure, even though the pain of losing her mother was still fresh. Why would Judy do something that put everything in jeopardy?

Avery sat down heavily in his reclining chair and heaved a long sigh. "I don't know why I told you that. I let the cat out of the bag. It's just that—Judy wants to adopt you and Mara, and she wants to be sure that no one will object."

It was Shoshanna's turn to sit down. "Adopt us?"

"Yes. But I wasn't supposed to say anything until everything was finalized. Judy didn't want you and Mara getting disappointed."

"So we'd live here? Permanently?"

"Yes. With Judy. And me, for now. And when I leave this house—well, the farm will belong to you all."

Shoshanna put her hand on Avery's arm. "Don't even think about that, Avery. You'll be here for a long time because we're going to take such good care of you."

"You do take good care of me, and I appreciate it," Avery said. "But I'm not going to say any more. I've spoiled enough surprises for one day."

Shoshanna walked back to the barn, reassured that the thing she cared most about—staying at the farm with the people she loved—seemed to be happening. The only cloud on the horizon was the worry that she feared she'd always carry with her—the worry that, someday, Adam would somehow find them and take them back.

CHAPTER THIRTEEN

Judy got back from town hall looking slightly weary and pensive. She went right to the sink and started rinsing a head of lettuce—and began yelling at a bird that seemed to be intent on eating the feed for the chickens out of the trough.

"Hi, Judy," Shoshanna said. "How was town hall?"

"Shosh! Hey. Listen, could you call Mara in? I have a couple of things to tell you. I think we should all sit down."

They all sat around the kitchen table. Judy looked so serious that Shoshanna's heart began to pound. What if her grandparents in New York wanted them to move there and live with them? Maybe that was why she looked so solemn.

"What's wrong, Judy?" Mara asked. "You're making me scared."

"Shhh, Mare," said Shoshanna, trying to stay calm herself. "Let Judy talk."

Judy took a deep breath. "Okay. First, I called your grandparents. Their names are Rose and Sid, and they live in a place called Queens, in New York. They sound like very nice people."

"We won't live there," said Shoshanna. "Even if they're nice. Even if they have tons of money."

Judy just looked at her. "You should think about this. Your mom was their only child. She was smart and beautiful, just like you two girls, and they loved her very much and pinned all their hopes on her. Then she met Adam, and everything fell apart. She dropped out of high school and started to get involved with drugs. Adam was not only a drug dealer and a thief, he also abused your mom. But you know that."

Shoshanna nodded. "She still loved him, though. That's what she told us. That's why she stayed with him."

"At first, yes, but after a while, no. She loved you two," Judy said. "You two are the reason she stayed. Not Adam. She left as soon as she could get you two out safely."

Shoshanna suddenly remembered Adam's conversation with Reed. That she, Shoshanna, was almost ripe. The way Ella didn't react but just took it all in. How even though she was scared and the risk was great, she was not going to let that happen to her daughter.

Mara and Shoshanna both found themselves thinking about Ella, and both found their eyes filling with tears. Judy cried along with them. "I'm sorry to make everyone so sad," she said. "We'll miss your mom for as long as we live and I'm glad you understand just how much she sacrificed for you. But the thing is, your grandparents have sold their house and they're moving to a one-bedroom apartment in Florida. Their health hasn't been great over the past few years, and they would love to raise you, but they don't think they are strong enough to, at this point in their lives."

"So what happens next?" Shoshanna asked.

"I wanted to adopt you, but legally, I knew I had to try to get in touch with your father," Judy said.

"Is he coming here?" Mara asked, eyes wide.

"You can't let that happen," Shoshanna said. "No, Judy."

"Nothing's going to happen, Shosh," she said. "Your father's dead."

The girls sat there, stunned into silence.

"I'm sorry to have to tell you like this. Today, I went to the police station to ask them to run a background check on your father because I knew that we'd have to tell him about your mom to go through the adoption process. They contacted the police in Oregon, and that's when I found out that he died several months ago. He died of a drug overdose. He was never even in California."

"So my mother really couldn't have seen him in her hospital room," Shoshanna said.

"Maybe she saw his ghost," said Mara.

Shoshanna started to cry.

"I know this must be hard to hear," Judy said.

Shoshanna shook her head. "No. It's not that. It's just that…Mara's right. She did see his ghost. So did I. So did Mara. His ghost haunted us every day."

"We can rest easy now," Judy said. "Adam's ghost is gone. But you do, however, have me. I'm a happy person, and I love living here on the farm. Avery's wonderful. My life is full. The only thing I wish I had but don't have are children of my own. Now, the doctor told me long ago that I couldn't have any, but that doctor didn't count on you two. So, what do you say? What do you think about us three—well, four if you count Avery, which I do—trying to make it as a family?"

Shoshanna looked at Mara and grinned. They threw their arms around Judy and held on. "I take it that's a yes," Judy said. "Your grandparents want you to visit, and I know you'll want to get to know them, so maybe you can visit when we can get the money together. They will be so happy to see that their beautiful and brave daughter isn't lost but very much alive in her daughters. And I know I will never replace your mom, and as they told me at town hall I'm on the young side, but I believe I can be a good mother to you both."

Shoshanna looked at her and grinned through her tears. "Does Avery know we're family?" she asked.

"I think he's felt that way for a long time, but today it's official," Judy said, smiling.

"Can we have a party?" Mara asked.

"Definitely," Judy said. "How about dinner at the Half Moon Diner? We'll put a candle in the pie. And we have to make it an early night, because tomorrow you two ladies have your first day of school." Shoshanna and Mara wasted no time running across the yard full tilt to find Avery. Mara was surprised when Avery started to cry, but Shoshanna wasn't.

On the way home from the diner, all of their bellies full of biscuits and potatoes and a particularly perfect candle-topped deep-dish peach pie, Shoshanna looked out the car window and saw the moon racing alongside the truck. She thought back to the night they'd left Sweet Earth and remembered the moon that night and the feeling they were being pursued. Tonight, Mara's head rested against her shoulder. Shoshanna caught Avery's eye. "That's a full moon there," he said. "A harvest moon."

"I used to think the moon was chasing us," Shoshanna said.

"I prefer to think it's keeping us company through the night," Avery said. Maybe he was right, Shoshanna thought. Maybe it was all in how you looked at it. And when the car pulled into the driveway, Avery bid them good night. "See you in the morning," he said.

Judy and Mara and Shoshanna stood for a moment in the moonlight and wrapped their arms around each other, then walked toward the barn. The kitchen light had been left on, and it shone like a beacon. Shoshanna turned to look at Mara's smiling face and offered up to her mother the swell of gratitude that suddenly flooded her heart. *Thank you for staying with us all the way. Thank you for getting us here safely. Most of all, Mama, thank you for bringing us home.*

ACKNOWLEDGMENTS

I would like to thank my beautiful family—husband, Sam, and children, Hannah, Jake, Rachael, Sarah, Eliza, and Micah, for their unflagging support and boundless love.

Thank you too to my stellar agents, Peter and Sandra Riva, for their sage advice and for believing in me from day one.

ABOUT THE AUTHOR

Laura Hurwitz lives in New Haven, Connecticut, with her husband and her six grown children (when they come to visit). She has been writing for as long as she can remember and was frequently disciplined in school for passing notes in class. Her first published works were travel-essay books about locations as distant as South Africa and as close to home as Nantucket Island. She is coauthor of the Adventures of Riley children's book series. When not writing, Laura is happiest reading, running, or doing yoga. *Disappear Home* is her first novel.